Y0-BRR-474

Sandra Nicholls lives and works in Ottawa, Ontario. Her first book of poetry, *The Untidy Bride*, was short listed for the Pat Lowther Award, and her second, *Woman of Sticks, Woman of Stones*, won the Archibald Lampman Award. She also took third prize in the International Stephen Leacock Poetry Competition. This is her first novel.

And the seas shall turn to **lemonade**

A novel

Sandra Nicholls

And the seas shall turn to **lemonade**

Amy!
May you
enjoy the
salt sea air
in this book!
Sandra
May 2012

Sandra Nicholls

ISBN: 098687700X
ISBN-13: 9780986877001

Cover design by Eric Quesnel
Cover photo: iStockphoto, File 1652152

For Dad

Acknowledgments

I am grateful to many people who helped me with this book, but first, I must acknowledge Charles Fourier (1772–1837), whose Utopian ideals inspired and informed my own vision of Tabitha and Nathaniel's story.

I thank all those who read the manuscript and commented, especially Mark Frutkin and Diane Schoemperlen, who kindly gave of their time and provided me with pithy blurbs for the back cover. I would also like to thank Joy Gugeler for invaluable editorial guidance. My thanks also to Nadine McInnis and the members of the Ottawa Writing Group, who gave me the kind of support and faith that all writers need. My gratitude extends to Anne McDermid, my agent, who believed in the book from the very beginning and who worked hard to promote it. Many thanks also to my colleague Eric Quesnel, for designing an awesome cover, and to Lauren Walker and Caroline Shaughnessy, for help with editing and formatting. A special thank you to Sylvain Bélanger, for his enthusiastic reading of the book and insightful suggestions.

I also wish to acknowledge the financial assistance of the Ontario Arts Council, the Canada Council and the City of Ottawa.

And finally I am deeply grateful to my family – to my husband Roddy Ellias, for his wise commentary on the book and his unwavering love and support, to my daughter Ellie, for teaching me by example the courage to follow my own path, and to my mother Bunny, for believing I could do it.

"We were all a little mad that winter. Not a man of us that did not have a plan for some new Utopia in his pocket."

Ralph Waldo Emerson, 1841

"*The experiences of my own life have left me painfully aware of how little counsel exists for the man of today concerning the modern universe! How blindly we enter in! Then there is the question of basic household management! To whom do we turn? Beset with the faults, foibles and follies that characterize us as human beings, we remain isolated in our respective households, prisoners of rational, but less than comforting individualism. But take heart. Apply yourself to the principles espoused herein. There is an alternative.*"

From *Everyman's Guide to the Modern Universe and Household Management*, Nathaniel P. Speck, Professor of Medieval History, St Simons University, Chisholm, Nova Scotia

One

Tabitha Black came from a long line of listmakers, all of them women, all of them miserable in love. Clever, pale-skinned, and stung by men for generations, they sought refuge in the ordered world of lists so skillful and so odd in their design only another Black would recognize them. After six weeks of sleeping with Jean-Pierre, Tabitha was making her way, theoretically speaking, through elementary school teachers, and both the man and the list were coming to an end. Mr. Varty, the Latin teacher, stalked her one morning as she rolled around under the satin sheets she'd ordered from an expensive catalogue, trying not to decline verbs out loud. Jean-Pierre pulled his lips back in what was meant to be an expression of pleasure but which could have passed as a sneer, and Tabitha, opening her eyes for a while and expecting to see the steamy black-rimmed spectacles of Mr. Varty instead saw the gap between Jean-Pierre's front teeth. (Was that what she had found so sexy about him, or did she have to confess it was merely his accent: "I understand you teach poleetical science.") Jean-Pierre began his thrusting in earnest, while Tabitha slid about on the sheets and the spectre of Mr. Varty hovered over them, musty and sexy as the first teacher you have a crush on, a dim lust that smells like chalk and gymnasiums.

"Tabitha, what's the matter?" Jean-Pierre turned over and reached for his rare Russian cigarettes. "Sheet."

"Did you say 'sheet'?" Tabitha giggled from under the bedclothes.

"Well, fuck then, whatever you English people say."

More titters and snickering. "I'm sorry, I can't concentrate."

"Tabitha, I think it's finished." The last syllable came out like "shed," and there was no stopping the laughter now. It was beyond all reason. But it wasn't like Tabitha to mourn the death of a relationship, since she had long ago given up the hope that love might strike her twice in a lifetime.

"You know, Tabitha, I always had it in my mind that one day we might live together – little cottage by the sea, kiddies running around, and all that."

Tabitha rolled her eyes.

"You must know it wouldn't work."

Jean-Pierre nodded thoughtfully, gazing at a crack in the wall.

"Pass me a cigarette, would you?"

They decided to puff away any bad feelings. Induced by the exotic smoke, they conjured up their private visions of lost love in companionable silence: waiting alone at frozen railroad stations in various but always remote places; taking off on airplanes; or disappearing into the black interiors of taxicabs. Their spirits rose for a while, as they aligned themselves with their inevitable loneliness (so romantic in the abstract), and then they began some discussion of who would be the new Chair of the Political Science Department. The bells of morning mass pealed away in the distance, calling to order the righteous of small-town Chisholm.

"Well, not Poolsey, for sure not Poolsey." Tabitha flicked some ash on to the floor.

"Why not? He's been there for years."

"The Dean hates him."

"Why?"

"Poolsey's got a bigger house."

"Ah. How very uncollegial. Then it's got to be Jackson."

Jean-Pierre got out of bed and began sweeping the ashes with a small silver broom and pan. Tabitha watched him for a while; she had to admit he was awfully sexy performing this menial task. She flicked again directly at his feet.

"Or Speck."

"Nathaniel Speck? Mister Medieval? Are you kidding?"

"My money's on Speck. He's been here forever, he's writing another bestselling book of useless theories, and he's disposed of that flea-infested beard for good."

Tabitha was out of bed now too, doing callisthenics by the window. She peered at Jean-Pierre from between her knees. "Mark my words, Jean-Pierre." She pointed her perfectly white bum in his direction and grinned. "Speck's time has come."

Tabitha's specialty was an obscure nineteenth-century Utopian socialist named Charles Fourier, who Tabitha studied with a kind of rapt adoration. No matter to her Fourier had been roundly denounced by her colleagues as a kook. She understood him as others hadn't. He was, after all, one of the first radical feminists! He knew that passions could be celebrated and fulfilled through social interaction – the absence of guilt and the organization of genuine freedom! And, as she'd point out, narrowing her blue eyes during a lecture, who can argue against the place of the series in nature? The harmony of the spheres? Who? Who?

Tabitha was a woman drawn like a magnet to Fourier's endless lists, and his theory that complete liberation of the heart and soul was possible, with the right social mechanisms. Tucked into her frozen little heart was a fervent desire for something that would vivisect the meaninglessness of all that she perceived around her – there could exist a new social order! People could live in harmony! There were no less than 810 personality types in Harmony, the Utopian Stronghold envisioned by Fourier, their days governed by the demands of the "Butterfly Passion" for constant change: five meals, eight kinds of work, choices, choices, choices. And, as the lecture notes tucked into her black leather portfolio explained, no ridiculous limitations imposed by the impossible demands of monogamous marriage, and it did not escape Tabitha's eye that ridiculous, impossible, and monogamous formed a rather symmetrically pleasing series themselves.

Her particular favourite, next to the *Scale of Misfortunes in Married Life*, was the *Hierarchy of Cuckoldom*, arranged progressively by category, type and species. These were the lectures her students loved, as she tossed from her mouth the flowers of wit Fourier had passed down to her: *The Vulgar or Grubby Cuckold; The Fulminating Cuckold; The Condemned, the Reciprocating, or the Swaggering*. On and on she listed, charming, chatty. A real spellbinder, as her mother would have said, and her students fell like flies. (*Cuckolds in the Bud*).

How neat it all was, how perfectly reasonable.

She was off to deliver one of these lectures, ripping down the halls of academia, black mini-skirted tunic, black tights, and running by in her head a list of all the impossibly uncomfortable red high-heeled shoes she had bought in her life, when she ran smack round a corner into Jean-Pierre.

Peering into the gap between his teeth and for a moment forced to admire his cool grey eyes, she thought first of a sassy comment, and then stopped, because she noticed he was wearing a cardigan, a comfortable old cardigan, a droopy, soft and snuggle-up-into sort of cardigan, and her heart was drowned in sadness. She watched him walk down the hallway, fearing that there would never be a man she would go home to at night, never in a thousand years, and then she saw the years laid out like rungs in a ladder, the ladder descending into a bottomless cavern, and a dark hopelessness took root in Tabitha's heart.

Tabitha was born of the first of many potential fathers. Dragged from one man's house to another, she soon lost the art of trying to begin again, watching her mother's failed attempts first with sympathy and finally with a cool kind of contempt. The rhythm of hoping, rising steadily inside her child's heart like a bubble in a tube, and then sliding back down again, had become too hard to bear. It was easier to give up hoping entirely. And Rosa Black was little help. She silenced Tabitha's childish questions about life with replies born of her own disappointments.

> *Is there life after death?*
> Who cares when you're dead?
> *Is there a God?*
> You really have to ask?
> *Where do babies come from?*
> Mistakes.
> *Do I have to change schools again?*
> Yeah, think of it as a learning experience.
> *Is this home now?*
> Ask me tomorrow.

Tabitha grew tall, and bookish, and almost got married to a man whose idea of a list was bread and milk, stuck to the fridge by a magnet. When that didn't work out, (*Disparity of Tastes and Personalities*, Fourier informed her later), she settled for tall and bookish, and graduate school opened its hoary old arms to welcome her in.

Tabitha had only really fallen in love once, during a summer course in Anarchist Politics. The course was offered in Hope, a town set in the middle of the Rocky Mountains. She remembered the way people there seemed to look straight through you to a point beyond their reach, far over your shoulders, past the dimly lit insides of the pool hall, past the Laundromat and its busted washing machines, past Wu Fats Chinese Food Emporium. Hope itself seemed to have been aptly named, as the long, blank stares of its inhabitants suggested – stretching past the claustrophobia of the mountains across to the plains, to that flat, whistled down expanse of bone-coloured wheat where all things were possible and a different future could be spread before you like a tablecloth.

There, at the mouth of the Fraser River, squeezed between two mountains, love had crept up and surprised her. She thought it had happened the first night Paul invited her to stay over at his apartment. Tall, and blond and Nordic looking, she could hardly believe he had fallen for her at all, because all the women had been crazy for him and she was sure he wouldn't be interested. But something in her lanky, lazy-eyed stare had caught his attention and she held it fast. Paul was an archaeologist who wanted to be a poet. He showed her how to chip away at rocks and make arrowheads, a skill she thought might one day come in handy for something.

His apartment was filled with fossils and rocks, but everything was pristine and neat, arranged for complete comfort and practicality. His single bed was tucked in a corner of a large L-shaped room, a single reading light on the wall above it, a red wool blanket tucked neatly into the folded corners. There were two tin cups in the cupboard and a teapot, two plates, two of everything it seemed, and plenty of camping gear. His knapsack hung from the rack near the front door, and there was a brick and board shelf affair along one whole side of the room, filled with books on Canadian history, folklore, and which mushrooms you could eat and which ones to avoid. There were no ornaments, except perhaps the odd feather, or a fat pinecone.

Paul had been so earnest in his pursuit, Tabitha had been caught completely off guard. He invited her round for dinner, surprised her with an appetizer of fried garlic cloves, so sweet she thought he must have been joking about what they were. They devoured an entire salmon, then took a shower together, wanting to feel the water running down their bodies, wanting to come together as new. Paul carried her to the small bed and turned out the light. Suddenly the sky above her was filled with a million constellations – Paul had mapped out the whole ceiling and most of the wall with glow in the dark stars. The surprise of those stars and the sudden thrust of Paul inside her made Tabitha crazy with pleasure and delight. It had been a long time since anyone had genuinely roused her, and she fell, right then, into a swoon of impossible love.

The love affair lasted all summer. They talked non-stop, about everything, slurping Shanghai Surprises and other sickly sweet drinks from Wu Fats, waiting for their laundry to spin dry at the Laundromat, tucked like spoons in Paul's bed, counting the stars. Until one night.

"Tabitha, there's something I've been wanting to say to you."

The two of them were lying pressed together in the bed, holding hands. Paul propped himself up on one elbow and stared down into Tabitha's face, stroking back her hair to reveal the high expanse of forehead which he so admired. Tabitha lay back blinking, almost embarrassed by the pure lust she felt for him, the absolute desire. The way he set it up, she was expecting a proposal.

"I think you are probably the most wonderful thing that ever happened to me." Tabitha went to speak but he carried on quickly. "But I just don't feel the same way anymore." Tabitha was confused for a moment by what he'd said. It still could have been a proposal, couldn't it? Did he feel differently, did he want to get more serious? Then she saw by the expression on his face that what he'd been trying to say was that he didn't love her anymore. That was it. She could barely breathe.

"I don't know what to say. It just went away. I just don't feel the way I should feel about you." Then he turned his broad Nordic back away from her and started to get dressed.

Tabitha stared around at the orderly little apartment, suddenly sensing its refusal to be crowded. Perhaps she was just too messy, too cumbersome – there was no rack or shelf large enough to contain her. Even in the little bed she began to feel huge, like an elephant trying to disguise itself under a sheet. There was really nothing she could say, nothing to come back with. He'd even complimented her, for Christ sake. She put her clothes on quietly and slunk away from the apartment, like a rat. The most wonderful thing that had happened to him. The words clung to her like a curse.

And so did seduction begin to take on an intoxicating whiff of revenge. Thank God she had escaped Paul's clutches, as she now began to think of it. Fourier's words rang in her ears: *"Is there any game of chance more frightful than an exclusive and indissoluble tie on which you stake a lifetime's happiness or unhappiness?"* Good God. One of the most popular of Tabitha's lectures, at least among her more thoughtful students, was the lecture in which she discussed Fourier's views of marriage and the family system. He had already documented on a sliding scale the various misfortunes of married life:

1. Chance of unhappiness
2. Disparity of tastes
3. Complications
4. Expense
5. Vigilance
6. Monotony
7. Discord in education
8. Jobs and dowries
9. Departure of children
10. Disappointing in-laws
11. Incorrect information
12. Adultery or cuckoldry

To these Tabitha had added her own.

13. Fear of commitment
14. Excessive criticism
15. Madness

And she was working on the list all the time. Her experiences with men represented a seemingly inexhaustible wellspring of new misfortunes to be added.

In Chisholm, Tabitha had at least found a purpose. Chisholm was where she intended to establish the first, working, Fourierite community in history. She had already purchased the land, twenty acres of it. The property was gnarled and spotty, full of unexpected hillocks and groundhog holes, trees bent sideways from the constant wind off the ocean, and no real pathways. There were scrap barren patches, where it seemed nothing was ever destined to grow except listless yellow grass, a marshy area even the beavers had abandoned, and a small, but miraculous wooded section right in the middle that Tabitha had nicknamed Cradle Island, for here all the trees seemed to bend inward, like protective parents over a cradle, and once inside, scarcely any light could penetrate the embrace of those trees.

But the scattered patchwork of nature's bounty wasn't what Tabitha saw when she walked around the property. For every tree, she conjured up a building, for every boulder, the barracks of Harmony. Here, an agricultural sector, there, a library. And, where the island of trees now stood, she pictured the Central Hive, the hub of the community, abuzz with life and conversation. She drew out maps, and architectural designs, a blueprint for the phalanx that Fourier had never lived to see carried out. Her heart was a rumble of planning and activity.

The land met all of Fourier's expectations for a truly workable community. Tabitha listed the requirements in a notebook and checked them off in red.

A tract of land at least three miles square.
Check.
A stream of water running through.
Check.
Intersected by hills.
Check.
Contiguous to a forest.
Close enough.
Right next door to Nathaniel Speck's place.
Well, you can't have everything, can you?

The population of Chisholm was about 2,000 people, in the summer. During the university year it swelled to 4,000, and the town split off two ways. St Simons, the rest of the town. The university was hardly a welcome presence. Virtually everyone at St Simons was from away, noses in the air, as any self-respecting local knew. Chisholm folk were farmers, miners, fishermen, practical people with their feet firmly grounded who liked to raid the used clothing bins at Frenchy's and buy their supplies at the Five and Dime down on Main Street. The faculty of St Simons did their shopping in Halifax, except when they were forced to buy something in town, and they almost completely supported the local health food store, and the coffee shop, where students and teachers alike gathered for a latte and a spot of atmospheric urban gloom on a bright winter's afternoon in Chisholm. Chisholm, Nova Scotia. One main street. Four restaurants (if you counted Tim Hortons.) Six churches, all Catholic.

When Tabitha first arrived in Chisholm, five years before, she had been enchanted. In the centre of town most of the houses were fairytale style, all towers and walkways, pastel colours with lazy front porches that curved around to the sides and purple lupins growing in bright profusion everywhere. On Main Street you could park all day for a quarter. The streets were wide and quiet and no one seemed to drive fast. People actually stopped their cars to let her cross. The university itself was an old Jesuit school – grey stone hauled from quarries near the sea and tiny turrets and leaded windows, the whole stately affair crawling with ivy. Two newer buildings had none of the old world charm about them but they were spacious and well maintained, and from most windows you could at least see the former splendour of St Simons, and breathe in its comforting aura of hard work and moral fortitude. The Political Science Department was housed in one of these two buildings, along with Philosophy, Sociology, and the newly formed Women's Studies. Tabitha's office was in a corner, and her window extended all the way around, so that she could watch the rugby games on the football field from one angle and watch the comings and goings of her colleagues in the parking lot from the other. Professor Dearing, the present Chairman of the Department, drove a massive (and ancient) champagne-coloured Mercedes Benz, and she loved to watch it as it edged its burly way into the parking spot reserved for the Chair. Dotted around were mostly Hondas and Toyotas and of course Jean-Pierre's bright red Karmann Ghia, also a relic, but beautifully maintained, and fast.

Tabitha came to St Simons straight out of university, after her mother's death. Everything had been a welcome distraction – the name plate on her door, "Professor T. Black," a lecture hall full of students, a vote at departmental meetings. Her mother had died accidentally, from botulism, after a summer of jam making. Tabitha remembered the heat rising from the steaming pots, the jewelled colours of the fruit as Rosa poured the jam into jars, the satisfying twist of the lids that, as it turned out, weren't quite as tight as they should have been. Tabitha had been just about to raise a piece of buttered toast smeared with jam to her lips when her mother started seeing double and slowly began sliding off her chair. Tabitha thought her mother was having a stroke, dropped her toast, and called 911. She sat in the front of the ambulance in a blur, trying to answer the paramedic's questions while listening for her mother's voice in the back. But there was nothing, only a horrible silence, and once Tabitha realized there were no sirens going, everything shifted into slow motion, the ambulance seemed to crawl towards the hospital, and even her words came out like heavy syrup, the shapes and weights of their syllables and consonants strange and unfamiliar.

Her mother was transferred almost immediately from the bright and hopeful glare of the emergency wing to the dim, subdued lighting of the funeral home, where lank strangers dressed in black suits kept telling her she had decisions to make. Later that night she paced all over the empty house, wondering who she should call, who would help. There were no siblings, there was (currently) no husband, and there certainly was no father around. Tabitha wasn't even sure who her father was. She tried to feel something, but inside was only a grim emptiness. She had stuffed sadness into so many pockets growing up it was impossible to find it. So she took action instead – called the funeral home, made all the arrangements, and sent her job application to St Simons with the morning post.

But one feeling remained. Tabitha could never shake the guilt that held her in its grip long after her mother was gone. She was the one who had insisted on her mother making jam in the first place. She had carried the idea around with her like a talisman ever since she was a child, remembering the way she had felt playing hide and seek at a friend's basement and coming across the shelves lined with provisions, jar after jar labelled and lightly frosted with dust, the idea of permanence, sustenance, planning ahead for the winter. It was an irresistible idea to Tabitha, and she had nagged and nagged her mother to buy the supplies. Rosa complied, and Tabitha's world was turned upside down. Her quest for permanence had left a permanent hole.

The lustre of professorship began to fade in the first year, especially as winter hit, early, and hard, the seemingly endless snow obscuring the view from her windows and the deep cold rendering her car a frozen torture chamber most of the time. Tabitha had been unable to purchase one of the "fairy" homes that nestled close to the university, because they were passed on from generation to generation of Chisholmites, and seldom went up for sale. Instead she had been forced to buy a plain somewhat featureless bungalow in the "suburbs," two minutes up the road. The house was painted a pedestrian pale blue, with a black roof and a black door, like a child's drawing. Vast plains of grass surrounded the house on all sides, except where the grey tongue of a driveway drew a line between her and her neighbour. Inside, the walls were a monotonous landscape of beige. There was no grace to the house, so sense of decorum. When you walked through the front door you were almost immediately, embarrassingly, right in the heart of the house. There was no coat cupboard, no vestibule, only a series of crude brass hooks set along one wall. The main bedroom was at the back of the house, vast and always chilly. By contrast, and as ample evidence of the complete lack of design, the bathroom was small and square, and she bumped her knees on the edge of the sink whenever she sat down on the toilet. She remembered thinking, when the real estate agent showed her around, that the whole business of living there would probably hasten her death. But she had got the job quickly, she had to move quickly, and she imagined she would be spending most of her time at the university anyway, so she filled it with her things, but it was never really home, if she in fact knew what that meant.

Tabitha's friends were the other odd single women who lived in the same, small university town because there were no jobs elsewhere. Some of them, unlike Tabitha, had succumbed to small town life. Ella, from Physics, chain-smoked her way through a nervous breakdown and departmental meetings, arguing that men and women should live in separate houses. Hope, in Theology, became so mild-mannered that she had taken a drop in her salary because the Dean told her the Football Team needed some scholarship money. Tabitha had eight members of the team in her Survey Course on World Politics. When they did manage to show up for class they sat together in a line at the back, their caps turned backwards on their heads and their hands scrunched down in their pockets, smirking. Although there may have been hope for one or two of them, she dubbed the lot of them The Offensive Line and tried to forget about them, especially alone at night, fidgeting under her silken sheets.

Some of her friends were married. The women would gather at Tabitha's house for wine and talk, listening to Michelle Shocked and Ferron, always starting out on chairs and couches and ending up on the floor, huddled, wanting the closeness, needing to ground themselves with other women. They all took their turns carping about men, but late at night, when the married women had to leave, the single women opened more wine and moved closer together, deeply suspicious of marriage, but not wanting to face their empty beds.

The last time the group got together Tabitha started wondering aloud about who might join Harmony – about who might fit in to the community of like-minded souls that Tabitha had in mind. They started with the few available single men in the university.

"Now there's Simon MacCauley, in Geology. At least there's something solid about him." Ella put this forward but Hope, flushed with wine, was quick to retort.

"If you can stand the maggots in his beard!"

Names, departmental affiliations and humorous put-downs followed for a while, and no one, at least at first, was really paying attention to Tabitha, who had started drinking late in the afternoon and long before anyone arrived. She was crouched against a dragon pot, a huge tropical leaf above her head shading half her face in darkness, and she was talking to the pot. Somehow she forgot she was trying to size up recruits for Utopia.

"If Speck sees me in the burgundy silk, he's dead meat." She shifted her feet a little and raised her glass. "They're all putty, putty in my hands! Spengler, ooh the art critic, he can't resist black lace." By now a few heads were turning her way. "Jackson – Taffeta! Foolproof!" The room was silent, aghast. "Something military with brass buttons and Coombs will be eating out of my hands.

The Dean can be had with a girlish white blouse," and here she turned conspiratorially to the tropical leaf, "and a black bra!"

Eventually Tabitha couldn't stop at the single men, and she went on to the married ones, the ghost of Fourier and his unbridled passions at her side, and on and on, past her friends' secret heartthrobs, husbands, the entire male faculty, outlining in detail her wardrobe of seduction, until she passed out. No one, not even one of her single friends, bothered to turn out the lights or rinse the glasses or cover Tabitha with a blanket when they left. Fantasy was one thing, but Tabitha had worked things out in detail, pinning down what was meant to be shifty and fleeting, wrestling it to the ground like a tiger.

Overnight, Tabitha became a loner. She didn't know why, because when she woke up she couldn't remember anything. The outline of a dragon's jaw had been pressed into her cheek from sleeping against the pot, and there was a dark stain of red wine on the carpet. Strange and unnamed commitments kept her friends from coming over, and the little circle of women went belly up.

As for men, Tabitha believed there was not a man alive who could not be seduced, somehow. But while Rosa blamed it on emotional weakness or the occasional lapse of the heart, something she herself understood, Tabitha, like Fourier, blamed it on the evils of the social order itself. The problem was rooted in the whole notion of isolated households – ridiculous and limiting family units that repressed the passions and were instituted more for economic reasons than those of the heart. According to Fourier, the heart by its very nature wanted to turn outwards, form associations, and find communities. So what if Tabitha had longed to be part of one of those ridiculous and limiting units growing up – she was a child, what did she know? So Tabitha reasoned. What she needed now was to prove that Fourier was right. After all, ideas couldn't just walk out the door, the way men did. Her mother, and her grandmother before her, and probably long before that, had tried marriage as a way of shaking off the cursed tradition, but it never worked. It never worked because the Black family lack of faith poisoned every relationship from the start. Tabitha fulfilled the family prophesy with more than a little enthusiasm, at least until now, when the unexpected was about to enter her life, by way of the phone lines.

"Hi! Professor Black? I got your number from the university, I hope you don't mind. This is Laura MacDonald. From two doors down?"

Tabitha was looking out her front window and wondering which two doors, which way, which house?

"The yellow house, with the black shutters."

Tabitha, startled, wondered for a moment if Laura had binoculars, and stepped back from the window.

"How are you?" Tabitha said stiffly, most of her encounters with her immediate neighbours kept to an absolute minimum. For someone who planned to set up a modern day commune, Tabitha was surprisingly antisocial.

"Well, just fine, thanks. Look, I know you've been here for a while, and we haven't actually got together, but we wondered, that's Brian and me, we wondered if you wanted to come over for pie?"

For a weird moment Tabitha thought about the mathematical pi, and then wondered if it was some sort of card game, of which she knew nothing, and in the long silence that developed as she was thinking, Laura took hold of the situation.

"Well, I'll take that as a yes! We'll see you at 7:30 tonight." And clicked off.

There was no escaping it. At precisely 7:45, Tabitha arrived at the door of the MacDonald household. She had passed by the house a hundred times, walking down to the university or to Sobeys for groceries, wondering about what went on behind the Sears-perfect curtains. It was the neatest house on the street – all the flowers in the garden seemed to bloom at the same speed; Christmas, Halloween and Easter decorations went up precisely two weeks before each holiday; the windows were so clean you could get a headache from the reflected glare.

"Come in, come in, they won't bite."

Tabitha was ushered into a kitchen where two children were eating sticky jam tarts and staring at her as if she were an alien. Laura MacDonald thrust out her hand and introduced herself. She wore a pink gingham shirt and a jeans skirt, and her short, earnest blonde hair was pulled back from her innocent face with a band.

"Don't mind the kids, just sit anywhere. You want some coffee?"

"Great." Tabitha settled lightly on the edge of a chair that had been smeared with jam, and took a cup of coffee from Laura. She stared in wonderment at the metal percolator plugged into the stove, its little red light flashing in alarm. "You want a jam tart? I made the jam myself."

Tabitha recoiled so suddenly from the sticky sweet that was being waved in front of her she almost spilled her coffee. Then she remembered her manners. "No, no thanks."

Laura popped the tart into a resealable plastic bag and pressed it shut with one swift and well-practised manoeuvre. Mysteriously the children had disappeared.

"So, you're up at the university." From wherever you were, you were always "up" at the university, "up" suggesting somewhere at a considerable remove from reality. Tabitha marvelled at the compression of speech the Maritimes had come up with. "You're not from around here, are you?" was another masterpiece of minimalism, usually accompanied by a raised eyebrow.

"Yes. In Political Science." Tabitha tried to keep the capital letters out of her voice.

"My husband and I, we both went to St Simons. That's where we met. He was in business, I did biology." Laura smiled and began scrubbing the sticky fingerprints off the kitchen walls. "Not that I have time to do anything about it." Tabitha wasn't sure if she heard regret in this last statement or not.

Just then Laura's husband walked in through the back door. Tabitha saw at once that he was an ordinary man, with thinning brown hair and an ordinary man's shirt, ordinary glasses, ordinary shoes. He ran his family's dry-cleaning business, and on the side he was an investment counsellor, a kind of friendly family financial advisor, the kind you could offer a cup-of-coffee-to-and-meet-at-the-door-in-your-sweatpants-and-feed-the-dog-while-you-were-talking-to kind of advisor. He shook Tabitha's hand, and gave Laura a peck on the cheek. Laura pulled back.

"What have you been doing out there? You're covered in dust."

The three of them glanced down at the small pile of grey dirt that had gathered at his feet. Tabitha noticed the dust was in his hair too, and resting lightly on his eyelids, giving his whole appearance a fuzzy softness, as if she was watching him through a piece of gauze. Laura asked the question, but he turned to Tabitha.

"There was a lot of damage after the ice storm a couple of years ago. Cracked the foundation, loosened the shingles on the roof. I'm still trying to patch it up."

"What storm?"

"You don't remember? Freak winter storm of 2000. No electricity – lines were weighted down in ice, roads were so slippery you couldn't get anywhere – they closed the main highway except for emergencies."

Laura pulled a snapshot off the fridge and passed it to Tabitha.

"This was it. Main Street, Chisholm. Deserted, like a wasteland. Everything frozen solid."

Tabitha studied the photograph. Gradually a memory resurfaced – she had been at a conference in Toronto when the storm hit. There was an odd, ethereal kind of beauty to what she saw, the transparent bridges of the tree branches threaded together in an elaborate lacework of ice and snow, icicles hanging down like frozen grey beards. She'd seen similar photos, in *The Globe and Mail*.

"This is probably what will kill us in the end – the weather!"

Laura and Brian stared at Tabitha, and then at each other, puzzled. As Maritimers, Tabitha realized they were probably so used to the climate being part of life itself Tabitha's statement must have sounded as if it had dropped out of the sky. Just as she was about to explain herself, Brian cut in.

"Anyway, I'd better get out of these clothes. Laura hates it when I mess up her kitchen, don't you sweetie?" But Laura had already turned away and was putting the photograph back up on the fridge. Tabitha watched Brian as he left the kitchen gingerly, trying not to shake off any more dirt. She decided not to make any more alarmist predictions about the end of the world.

Later that evening, Tabitha wondered what it was about Laura's husband that had him poking into her mind, unbidden, and curiously unshakeable. There was nothing physical she could remember about him at all. He could have been made out of cardboard. Yet in the morning, she would wake up, call him, and make an appointment. It really was time she looked after her finances, she reasoned, and he was just down the street, and he did seem trustworthy. The motto of his company was "Little by Little," and she liked that, picturing her small clump of savings growing each year, little by little, her nest egg, as he called it, in an innocent and disarmingly homey fashion. And so, Brian MacDonald, first-born son and heir to his father's dry-cleaning business, came idling into Tabitha's life. The morning of the appointment she lay back in her bath and began, in an earnest kind of ecstasy, to list her assets.

"Just think of it as a savings account. You've got nothing to lose."

Tabitha watched Brian's brown, ordinary, thinning hair. (*Endearing, Helpful Cuckold*). She watched his pale, ordinary hands reach into a blue portfolio for some blank forms. Goose bumps formed on her arms. She pictured Rosa Black, peering down from some cloud, her three husbands beside her, calling out that it would never work. She pictured the words dropping out of the sky and breaking up just above her head, making no sense.

A persistent, nagging little thought of her own kept edging in. She tried elbowing it out, tried to focus all her energies on the man sitting across from her, shuffling through forms and papers, this home builder, hearth keeper, champion of her future. But Tabitha couldn't keep the question from creeping into her brain: could he be Harmony's first potential resident?

It was a gnarly problem she faced – how to find precisely the right occupants for Harmony – the 1,620 (810 personality types multiplied by two) members of her self-sustaining community. But this man? She knew it was a notion borne either of lunacy, or despair. After all, Brian conjured up a world of family picnics, barbeques in the back yard, a sensible bedtime at ten, the children washed and scrubbed and tucked up in their little beds, everything shiny and shipshape. The neatest of isolated households – a test case if ever there was one. If Fourier came through on this one, then she would prove for sure his theories were correct. If Brian MacDonald really was stifled by the boundaries of conventional marriage, then it was almost her duty to introduce him to the joys of harmonious association. Wasn't it? And she wanted to start with men, men who would help build the architecture of Harmony, the greenhouses and libraries, the dining halls and the schools, the pathways and the orchards and the workshops.

Suddenly Brian's voice interrupted her reverie.

"When you plan ahead, retirement can be like starting again! Just think about it."

Tabitha's eyes grew misty at the very thought. Perhaps the curse was about to be lifted.

"First of all, we'll do a computer profile of your assets and debits, get it all down on paper."

"Oh, I've done that already. I've prepared two lists." She handed him an immaculate set of numbers, banging her knees together under the table like an excited child.

"My, my. I am impressed." His eyes travelled over the orderly sets of assets and debits. "My, my."

Tabitha could barely contain her sense of anticipation. In an uncharacteristic fit of domestic fervour, she decided to invite Brian, Laura, and their children for Saturday dinner.

She spent Saturday morning at Sobeys. What did children eat? There seemed to be row after row of pre-packed foods with names she thought children would like: Snackables, Dunkaroos, Mini this and Mini that. She threw a load in the cart. She bought roast beef for the adults, which she would serve with a Béarnaise sauce, baby carrots and asparagus, Lyonnaise potatoes. And a small salad of mixed greens. The produce was so lousy at Sobeys it took her at least an hour to pick out the best of what was there. She selected what appeared to be a lovely English cucumber but when she went to pick it up her thumb squashed right through it. The lettuce was pale and anemic. The carrots looked ancient. Tabitha began to despair, but carried on regardless. Now that the wheels had been set in motion she had to go through with it. She could just bury everything in sauces and chopped parsley. At least it would look good on the plate.

Tabitha wondered if Rosa was looking down at her, in her suburban kitchen, unpacking groceries and planning a family dinner. At least Rosa knew how to cook; that was one thing she had taught Tabitha. She could whip up a sauce almost out of the air, crack eggs into a bowl with one hand, cook perfect pasta. During their better moments, Rosa and Tabitha would take turns breaking open eggs and pretending they were some of the men who had come into their lives. "Oops, there goes Costas." Crack. "And William." Crack. "And that icky little grocery boy who used to peer at us through the window." Splat.

She'd even managed an apron, a relic she'd found at the back of one of the drawers when she was cleaning up. It had tiny red ladybugs all over it, a dark blue background, and wearing it Tabitha thought she'd seldom looked more appealing.

As the doorbell rang Tabitha smoothed out her apron and flicked on a little more of the ultra-glossy lip polish she had purchased in Halifax the week before. When she opened the door Laura's two boys tore straight in and knocked over a candle she had set up on the coffee table, setting fire to the carpet. The flames shot up with alarming speed, a sulphuric smell curdled the air, and the boys took turns trying to put the fire out with the silk cushions from her wingback chair. They all stood transfixed as the boys whacked at the spot, until the acrid smell of burnt fibres finally roused Laura into action and she ran over and smacked them both around the ears. There was a small black hole in the carpet and black smears all over the silk cushions. Laura stared over in horror.

"I am so terribly sorry," she began, "so terribly sorry." Tabitha stepped in to assess the damage.

"It really doesn't matter," Tabitha said, although she had picked the cushions out especially from a very expensive catalogue to go with the colours of her chair. "What's a couple of cushions?" Indeed, what were four squares of silk brocade stuffed with poly-foam next to the object of a major social experiment?

Tabitha and Brian managed to reposition the coffee table so that it hid the black hole in the rug, and Laura promised to sew up a couple of cushions that she promised would be just as nice.

"Now, let's have a drink to celebrate, shall we?" Tabitha was feeling so festive it was slightly unnerving for her guests, who were still feeling awful about the whole burnt mess. "I've picked out an endearing little red wine for us. Shall I pour?"

"Oh, a beer for me, if you've got one," Laura said.

Tabitha turned her head hopefully towards Brian, who seemed torn between the two women and the choice he had to make. Feeling a little lightheaded himself, he threw caution to the wind. "I'll try a drop of that."

Laura looked slightly betrayed, and Tabitha strode into the kitchen triumphant. She returned with a can of beer for Laura and a tulip-shaped crystal flute filled with red wine for Brian. The boys had disappeared into Tabitha's back yard, which was about the size of a football field. It was typical of the absence of design that characterized the outskirts of Chisholm – the smallest houses had the biggest lots. There was nothing in Tabitha's yard, just a long expanse of grass, but for children, it was paradise.

"Well, bottoms up." Tabitha remembered the last time she had used that phrase, and the upset that followed. "I mean, bombs away!"

For a while Brian and Tabitha talked about local politics, whether or not they should expand the highway, and why the local theatre never showed anything except *Rambo* and similar action films. It wasn't long before Tabitha introduced Fourier into the conversation. She directed her remarks at Brian, who tried to interpret them.

"So, let me get this straight. We're all alienated from our natural desires. Civilization as we know it is a crock."

Tabitha smiled at Brian's use of the vernacular.

"Exactly. What's so great about civilization? All civilization has given us is fraud, oppression, and carnage."

Brian looked confused.

"So what does he suggest then? A free for all?"

Tabitha leaned forward, her eyes glowing.

"No, no, not at all. A world where all the passions are respected, not repressed." She gave Brian a particularly penetrating stare. He looked uncomfortable for a moment, and then simply returned to his former thought.

"A free for all."

"It's not the same thing."

"Well, give me an example." Too much theory made Brian fidgety. He was a practical man.

"Okay, we all have the desire to compete, right? It's natural, am I right? But it can lead us into trouble."

"I suppose so."

"But what if we used that passion to produce, say, a better harvest – challenged teams of people to produce better fruit trees! For the benefit of all!"

By now Tabitha was so excited she could barely sit still. But ready as she was to talk about Fourier all night long, Tabitha realized they had both been ignoring Laura, and she decided to show off her grace and good manners by bringing her into the conversation. Besides, Brian didn't seem to be buying what she was saying. At least not yet.

"Well, enough political theory for one day!" She took a healthy swig of her wine and turned to face Laura. "So, you said you studied biology. Did you have an area of specialization?"

Laura pushed a stray lock of hair behind her ear. "Frogs."

Tabitha resisted the urge to laugh, giddy from the red wine. "Frogs?"

"Well, specifically their hibernation patterns."

Tabitha pulled herself up in her seat and felt a twinge of guilt. She was, after all, an academic herself, open minded, curious.

"Really. How fascinating."

Tabitha looked over at Brian, who had a glazed look on his face and was peering through his raised wine glass like a kaleidoscope. Laura ignored him, buoyed by the first glimmer of interest in her field of expertise to have been expressed for some time.

"I did a lot of research into freeze tolerance. Did you know that wintering tree frogs survive freezing by turning sixty-five per-cent of their total body water into ice? It's quite incredible."

Tabitha was, in fact, interested, but she didn't want Laura to take over the evening.

"I guess we all have our survival tactics! As for me, I'd rather go to Cuba!"

Brian smirked and giggled. "Yeah, me too. Besides, why don't you come up with something useful, like a poison to get rid of these damn grasshoppers."

A particularly dry summer in Nova Scotia had created an infestation of grasshoppers in the area, a fact Brian was painfully aware of, as his clients began to dwindle, fearing the loss of their crops and their income.

Laura drained her beer and continued, ignoring them both.

"This quality is unique, totally unique among vertebrates. But eventually, we might learn something from them. About human cryopreservation, for example."

Tabitha was having a hard time reconciling the domestic Laura with the brainy little scientist she suddenly seemed to have become. But Brian seemed determined to reduce everything Laura was saying to its lowest level.

"Well, I don't want someone freezing my nuts for the future! Jesus."

Brian had revealed a tacky, distressing streak, but Tabitha batted it away from her like an annoying fly.

Laura waved her beer bottle in Tabitha's direction, gesturing for another. Tabitha stepped into the breach.

"Well, I'd love to know more about it, Laura. Might come in handy some day."

Laura ignored her and stared at Brian. "You never have been able to deal with it, have you, the fact that I had a life too." Her voice was almost inaudible. "Before I got swallowed up in yours."

Laura clanged her beer can down on the coffee table and went to fetch the children. Tabitha tried not to clap her hands, having already uncovered cracks in the isolated household, without even trying. Despite the picture perfect exterior, the flower gardens, the holiday decorating, marriage obviously wasn't working, for either of them. She was plumped up with success, and for a few moments Brian and Tabitha were alone together.

Brian started to say something but Tabitha cut him off before he had a chance.

"You don't need to apologize. Conflict is inevitable in daily life." Tabitha couldn't believe what she'd just said. It sounded as if it had been lifted off a fridge magnet. "Well, you know what I mean."

"Tabitha, I did want to talk to you about something." The conversation had an eerie familiarity, and yet still Tabitha couldn't do anything about the sense of excitement and anticipation that began flushing through her veins. "Mutual funds or T-bills. Have you thought about which you'd prefer?"

Tabitha tried not to let her disappointment show.

"Whatever you think is best. Can I get you some more wine?"

As she walked into the kitchen Laura and the boys came in the back door, all talking at once, the children's faces streaked with dirt and grass.

"Into the bathroom and wash up." The children didn't move. Laura turned to Tabitha. "I'm sorry about earlier." Tabitha let her go on. "It's been a bit of a bad week."

But Tabitha couldn't be angry. She should get down on her hands and knees and thank Laura for what had come suddenly into her life – the life itself that had been breathed back into every waking activity. The premise of Harmony was finally taking shape – she would have the proof that Fourier had been right all along! The smug little household she had so longed for as a child was no more than society's prop. Tabitha's ridiculous longing for it had killed her mother, the only family she had ever had. From somewhere deep inside the labyrinth of cause and effect, she realized Laura was still talking.

"I think I'll take the kids home and get them washed up. You and Brian can finish up your financial stuff and then we'll come back."

Handed to her again on a silver platter. She returned to the living room.

"Now, what we need to consider, when preparing a personal financial plan," and here Brian stopped to look at Tabitha over the top of his glasses and clear his throat, "is what you really want."

Tabitha looked over and smiled. Brian cleared his throat again, jutting out his chin and pulling at the collar of his Chisholm plaid shirt.

"Where you want to be, say, ten years from now."

Tabitha snuggled into the seat beside him on the sofa and handed him his glass of wine.

"When you plan to retire."

"Of course," she said in a voice suddenly too loud, "when I plan to retire. Let me think."

"Take your time, Tabitha, there's no rush." At this command, uttered with her name in the middle, Tabitha felt a little swoon pass through her. "We can put together a variety of scenarios – a five year plan, a ten year plan. It's up to you, and your needs."

It all seemed so orderly, so contained. A five year plan. A ten year plan. Tabitha's heart leapt. He could be Harmony's accountant!

"I can come back when you've had a chance to think it over. You can fill out this questionnaire for me, and then we can discuss it."

Brian's wine sat untouched in the glass on the coffee table. His shirt draped unwrinkled over his chest. His shoes remained laced and enclosed over his feet. Tabitha began to see him as a kind of gift, waiting to be unwrapped. She began to examine him in this new light, wondering what she would find hidden there, and there, and beneath that fold. This was the thought that would contain her, make the time pass.

"Next week then? When you've had a chance to fill them in?"

Next week didn't sound so bad anymore, not so far away.

"Tuesday? Seven o'clock?"

Brian cracked open what appeared to be a brand new agenda book, with spaces to be filled in everywhere. To do, to phone, to write to. Daily, weekly and monthly objectives. Time slots for every half hour. Tabitha saw her name appear like magic in the little seven o'clock window, under a ladder of open spaces that extended until midnight, when the agenda book itself decided it was time to stop.

Avoiding the Evils of False Advertising

"There is no question that the mania for goods and services perpetrated by our extensive advertising culture is a paltry but pervasive substitute for genuine human feeling, a giant corporate fakery. Lacking in spirit? Buy yourself something. Pretend! Feeling empty inside? Buy a new wardrobe. Look the part! But try as we might to claw back a sense of authentic life for ourselves, a sense of meaning and purpose, we will never achieve it through the mail order catalogue or the latest flyer from Sears. We are fools to try. Saddened, disenfranchised, and very human, but fools, nonetheless."

From *Everyman's Guide to the Modern Universe and Household Management*, Nathaniel P. Speck, Professor of Medieval History, St Simons University, Chisholm, Nova Scotia

Two

Nathaniel Speck was about to begin his time-tattered lecture on "Women as Landowners in Medieval England" when he saw the black cloud approaching in the distance. His students saw it too, at almost the same time, and their heads turned in unison as Nathaniel shuffled the yellowed file cards in his hands, scribbles and arrows pointing every which way.

"Romance is one thing," Nathaniel attempted in his loudest and most attention-getting voice. "But when it comes to women and land in the middle ages..."

Seventy-five gum-popping, pencil-chewing, hormone-raging, condom-toting students continued to stare out the window.

"Under English common law," he tried again, "unmarried women and widows were on equal footing with men, at least as far as private matters were concerned." Nothing changed. "EQUAL FOOTING," he shouted.

Seventy-five open mouths, in profile. Nathaniel stared at the ceiling.

"Then there is the question of sex."

He looked back down and across the sea of faces.

"I thought that would get your attention. Now, let's continue, shall we?"

He steadied himself behind the lectern.

"The possession of land gave to women unprecedented power and position. And what was the other most important source of power for women?" Nathaniel went on to answer his own question. "The nunnery! For example, let's look at a prime example of how nunneries actually functioned…"

Suddenly a hand shot up in the second row.

"Yes, what is it?"

"You know, professor, they say that if you leave them in a field of turkeys they'll eat up all the feathers!"

Nathaniel sighed and removed his glasses, turned again towards the window where the black cloud was now a misty set of shadows.

"Mr. Rushford, what exactly are you talking about?"

"The hoppers!! It's just like in the bible!! Haven't you been reading the papers?"

"I am not particularly interested in modern media, Mr. Rushford." There was a crush of giggles. "Is there something I should be aware of?"

"Grasshoppers! They've been eating their way right across the valley. It's a freak of nature, sir."

All eyes turned again towards the black cloud, which Nathaniel now understood was a seething, hopping, gnawing, gnashing horde of uncontrolled arthropods bent on destruction. Insects of any kind made Nathaniel uncomfortable. He didn't like the way they moved, their speed, their spindly legs and squishy bodies, or the way they disappeared in a kitchen, then sprang out from behind a tin or skulked in the bottom of a cup. And here they were, making for Chisholm with alarming speed. Still, he tried to stay calm.

"Does anyone know the biblical reference Mr. Rushford is referring to?"

Nathaniel was trying, in a half-hearted way, to salvage something out of the lecture. A fat, miserable looking girl with a ring through her tongue, who always sat in the front row, waved her hand aimlessly in the air. Nathaniel nodded her way.

"Exodus. For the locusts covered the face of the earth and blotted out the sun. Etcetera."

"Good, Miss McDonald, good. And why exactly did God send down the plague to Egypt?"

"To get the Pharaohs to let the Hebrews go, man."

A young man with masses of blond curls had inserted the last answer, then turned and smiled leeringly at the girl next to him, who had a set of bangles on her arm that reached up to her elbows. It was okay to know the answer as long as you delivered it with a sneer.

Nathaniel seized his chance to re-enter the world of his lecture.

"And so it's all about land again, isn't it? The importance of land. Now let's get back to the lecture."

Nathaniel took a sip from his water bottle and cleared his throat, adjusted his weight behind the lectern, and got ready to speak. But another voice interrupted.

"You know in Pictou they didn't leave enough grass to feed one single cow."

Nathaniel looked up towards the back row where a young man in a baseball cap had his feet propped up on the seat in front of him and was chewing and smacking away at a piece of gum. He nodded his head and looked around at his classmates, satisfied he had their full attention. "They're like fucking eating machines man."

Nathaniel slapped down his note cards on the lectern with a bang.

"That will be enough, Mister McKewan. Enough interruption and enough profanity." But even as he spoke, Nathaniel knew he had lost them. The relentless cloud beyond the window was impossible to ignore, especially if you were seventeen and infatuated by chaos of any kind, at least, that's what Nathaniel reasoned. It was different for him, he was a serious intellectual, he had learned self-discipline and concentration on the task at hand. And so, undaunted by the prospect of a natural disaster, by its black looming presence beyond the window, Nathaniel stayed upright in his dedication to the rigours of study and hard work. As hordes of hoppers munched and gnawed their way through grass, crops, vegetables, even household wiring, Nathaniel led his wayward students through English common law, the custom of courtesy, the intricacies of feudal law, the complicated patterns of marriage and betrothals.

Nathaniel knew the lecture so well that he could easily be thinking of other things while he was speaking. Which he was. A new section for the sequel to his book: *Everyman's Guide to the Modern Universe and Household Management, Volume Two*. It was going to be right up to date. If it came out next year, it would sell like hotcakes! "Ridding the home of plagues of insects." Farmers would swarm the bookstores, homeowners would flock! Besides, there was only one minor glitch to the idea – how to actually do it. As he was speaking he was jotting notes on the papers sitting on the lectern: find out about grasshopper behaviour in groups.

"On the death of the husband, I might add, and by right of the dower, the widow was able to enjoy one third of any land seized during the marriage – for life." He continued scribbling: order Orthoptera, suborders Caelifera and Ensifera – what makes them tick?

"Because of the importance of land, marriages were often arranged while children were still in their cradles." Which species swarm? Why?

There was a loud and collective whoosh of paper as the bell went off and Nathaniel's students folded their notes and clapped their books together, slid out from behind their desks and began swarming towards the exit. Nathaniel was still scribbling when he became aware of a small figure standing beside the lectern. He didn't look up.

"Yes?"

"Professor Speck, I understand the weekly assignment but I may not be able to complete it for next week."

Nathaniel continued jotting.

"And why is that?"

"It's the grasshoppers, sir. My father, he has a farm out in the valley. We could be wiped out by next week."

Nathaniel looked up into the freckled face of the girl whose name he temporarily forgot.

"That's a bit of an exaggeration, don't you think?"

"No, sir. They're eating 300,000 tons of food a day, according to *The Herald*."

Nathaniel wrote down the figure in his notebook.

"Sir?"

Nathaniel looked up.

"Yes?"

"About the assignment?"

Nathaniel weakened as he looked up into her wide green eyes, temporarily distracted from his latest research project.

"Come and talk to me next class. Let me know how your father is doing."

"Thank you sir."

Nathaniel's eyes strayed over the stack of books his young student had piled in her arms. On its side he could see the spine of his own.

"How are you enjoying it?"

"Enjoying what?"

Nathaniel plucked the book from the stack and held it in front of her.

The girl looked mildly embarrassed. "Oh that, well, I actually bought it for my father. I haven't read it." She studied Nathaniel's face. "Yet."

Nathaniel marvelled at the author photo that graced the back cover, along with the solicitous quotes that had been obtained from some of his colleagues, on the understanding that he would prepare similarly saccharine praises for their books when the time came. The photographer had pinned Nathaniel in his office, set up an army of lights and what looked like umbrellas, had Nathaniel lift his chin, drop his eyebrows, try not to squint as he conjured up a look of professorial seriousness, mixed with just the right amount of down home practicality to boost sales. But Nathaniel knew who he was. Big, overweight, blustering, with ratty clothes and dishevelled facial hair. Yet when the photographer had sent the proofs, he had been astounded. For staring back at him then, and now from the back of his book, was a handsome, if not somewhat intimidating man, eccentric perhaps, but endearing, alluring, even sexy, if he dared think it. The marvels of airbrushing! Twentieth-century photography! Nathaniel placed the book back in his student's hands, and wondered who she saw when she looked at him, the man in front of her or the man in the photograph. What he couldn't have known was that despite his appearance, and it always surprised them, once the students reviewed their notes after class they discovered an elegant continuity of thought, a clarity that seemed at odds with the lumbering brute of a man who was at the source of it all.

By now the class had emptied and Nathaniel turned to the window. He was certain the students had over-dramatized everything, expanded the truth for effect. He hardly expected a plague of locusts in this day and age. There were scientists, computers, ways of dealing with things. Ways for other people to deal with things, especially. He could research, of that there was no doubt. And he could write it up too. But beyond that was the vast, misty, fog of theory, weighed down by inertia.

He wasn't normally lenient about class assignments, but something about the green-eyed girl had possessed him, taken him back to a vision of ecstasy he had experienced almost twenty-five years ago, in the house where he was born. Wide as well as tall, spacious, built before the turn of the century, the house was once his family's pride, and knitted into its construction were the secrets of Speck's ancestors, lusty, or cranky, or exotic by turns, the house shifting its silent gears with each succeeding generation.

That particular winter Nathaniel had turned fifteen. One evening, bored, he began walking the lengthy passages and corridors of the house, feeling the cross drafts that moved through the house, quick tongues of chill that penetrated under the windows and entered through cracks in the plastered walls. Nathaniel's older cousin, green-eyed Fiona, was visiting, but she had disappeared upstairs. The hardwood floors, polished and uneven, creaked with her footsteps. Nathaniel closed his eyes and pictured her moving from room to room, her elegant slippered feet, narrow with rosy painted toenails, the trail of her housecoat gliding behind her. Beyond the window of the study the trees stood mummified in burlap; Nathaniel opened his eyes and saw the pale lights from a distant house. There was water running in the upstairs bath.

From the bottom of the central staircase, Nathaniel studied the small stream of light that poured from the window above the bathroom door. He imagined steam and scent and something flowing green into the water, a woman's soft hands, and he crept up the stairs, up the thick red carpet that ran the length of the stairs, climbed onto the armoire at the top, steady, and softly now, he looked down, down through the clouds, as he breathed in the mystery of musk and flowers and his cousin Fiona.

The mystery of womanhood was about to be revealed. From the coils of steam a hand, a curve of breast, a tantalizing glimpse of rounded hip. Fiona stood in front of the mirror, tying her hair back with silvered clips. A cloud rose. Nathaniel saw the thin white stretch marks that cupped her stomach on either side like the petals of a tulip, thin tributaries that snaked like rivers. He saw her small, rounded breasts, which now and again would appear and disappear in the puffs of steam. He was mesmerized.

And so did Fiona, only twenty and already engaged to a Dick someone or other, become his vision of perfect womanhood, a vision he kept for nearly twenty years pinned to his heart, the cold breath of February each year turning Nathaniel Speck to fire.

Nathaniel left the classroom and headed for his own, special spot in the Fallow-Dickenson Library, and although it wasn't reserved in any formal way, everyone knew it was Professor Speck's table and respected his right to cover each square inch of its landscape with piles of tottering books and papers, much to the amused delight of his students, and the frustrations of the librarians who had to restack everything. It was a table under the North window, a chilly spot in the winter but set admirably between the reference section and the rare book room. It was under this very window, surrounded by stacks of paper and books and pencils, that Nathaniel had decided it was time to marry.

Six weeks had passed since the decision. He had been perched, under the mangled stained glass light of the North window, thinking about Genesis and preparing for his next lecture. Suddenly he noticed giant dollops of tears splashing on to his thighs, and he hurried to wipe them away. The solitary and often lonely business of research had been a steady companion for so long that he had almost forgotten what it was to need other people, but something about the light that day, the way it streamed like a series of bright arrows through the window, seemed to have pierced the armour of his feigned indifference. Suddenly there was no one to share his passion with, and suddenly there was a need to share it. Suddenly his theories of womanhood, which he had written about extensively and which had sustained him for so long, were no longer enough. Confused, he lurched out of the library, hoping no one would see him, and headed straight for the parking lot.

Breathing hard, Nathaniel tried to pull himself together in his car. He caught sight of himself in the rear view mirror and realized that if he was to attract anyone, his beard must be the first thing to go. Mangled, stiff, and scratchy as cheap plastic thread, it had been grown and nurtured for years in academic isolation. He grabbed the wire cutters he kept in the glove compartment and tried to hack most of it off, although it didn't take long to realize he would need a razor to finish the job, something Speck hadn't examined for years. And thus the quest had begun, with Speck hunched over the Pharmasave display, tufts of hair sprouting from his face as if he were the result of some cross-breeding experiment: old goat with university professor.

Speck had been fascinated with the advancements in men's shaving gear – moisturizing strips, tiny claws that set up beard hairs like blades of grass to be mowed down, flexible heads that dipped in and out where your face did. Living as he did, in relative isolation from the world of strip malls and fast food, he had remained delightfully unaware of many developments in technology. But privately he suspected that no man-made object could possibly match all the contours of his face. For that he needed softness, he needed a woman's hands, all lotioned and sweet-smelling, saying, without saying, "there, there," and in the dark silk of night, "there, there."

Looking up for a moment, he found himself face to face with Miss Feltmate, the new cosmetician. Well, she wasn't actually a cosmetician at all, but she'd read all the Avon catalogues from cover to cover for years, and although her own make-up was somewhat askew, owing to the fact that without her glasses she could hardly see, she knew a tube from a stick and could point customers to the right aisles for odd purchases like mineral oil (first aid? baby needs?) and so she was hired. Peering into her eyes all Speck could see were some faint smudges of green and the odd hoary eyelash, blackened and sticky and bent, trapped, desperately trapped, behind the thick lenses of her glasses.

"Dr. Speck, what have you done to your face?"

Nathaniel Speck was not an unkind man, and so he resisted the reply which sprang to his brain, and fortunately not to his lips, and he merely smiled, a wobbly, weak smile, and put his hand to his chin to stroke his beard, which was, as he had quite forgotten, not there.

"I will be searching for a wife." He cleared his throat. He began stroking the tufts on his chin. "I will need a razor."

Speck had a disarming habit of speaking the truth in public, and often at inappropriate times, such as last year's presidential dinner, when he suggested that the Archbishop's wife take some Valium, a suggestion he had only intended to be helpful. Nathaniel Speck would never again be invited to sit at the President's table, no matter how high the tolerance for eccentricity was at that select table.

"I see, I see." Miss Feltmate sputtered. "I see."

"Yes, precisely. That is why you wear glasses, Miss Feltmate." Nathaniel attempted a chuckle, and returned his gaze to the racks of razors, to their masculine, thrusting names, their masturbatory iambics: Actra, Sensor, Target. "Thank you, I think I can make my own selection." (Razors? Wives?)

In truth, Miss Feltmate saw nothing, nothing at all. For her, it was a clutter of straps and stockings, clumsy grabs, and embarrassed cups of tea in silent bedrooms while the clock ticked and tsked accusingly from the bedside table.

Miss Feltmate couldn't possibly have known how companionably inept they both were in the area of love. After purchasing the razor, Nathaniel hurried home, and there, with a growing despondence, he surveyed the rag and tatter nature of his kingdom. Floorboards and furniture paint splattered, splinter spears underfoot, old pails, stained undershirts, unmarked bottles of acids and chemicals, unfinished projects, broken tools, beetles and flies whorled in hair and dust, books, books, books. Speck lay back on the bed and rolled his eyes to the collection of jars behind his head. Twelve jars filled with dirt. (Things living in them once.) His belly flopped over ahead of him as he rolled over on his side. This business with the razors and the Pharmasave was all bravado. How would he find out what the modern woman wanted? How could he find a woman at all? Sure he'd written a book, but what did he really know? All he understood were things medieval, his specialty. All cloisters and visions. Women behind the cloud veil of myth and superstition. He stared over at the gnomic poem he had taped to the wall, the paper yellowed and torn, but the words still able to move him after so many years:

Dear is the welcome one
to his Frisian wife, when his ship is at anchor;
his boat has arrived and her man come home,
her own husband; and she calls him in,
washes his sea-stained rainment and gives him fresh clothes,
grants him on the land what his love requires...

Lying back on the bed Speck began leafing idly through the pages of the campus newsletter. And there it was, an advertisement hidden in the back classified section, somewhere between Student Apartments for Rent, and Gay Boy seeks Photographer for Artistic Pursuits:

Orange Blossom Girls from India
Pure Hearts/Exotic Beauties
For Marriage to Serious Persons Only
Write for Catalogue

For a week Speck had carried the ad around in his pocket, the phrase "Marriage to Serious Persons Only" being the most riveting, and there, in the breast pocket of his tweed jacket, the same one he wore day after day, season after season, it had somehow burned its way through that scant fabric and right through to his heart, where he began to believe it was possible.

He imagined himself a homesteader, a provider, after all, here he was a university professor – how much more serious could a person get? A big man with a house of his own. Her man come home. How she would come to appreciate his bulk and his earnestness, a small, tidy woman tucked into his bed, Speck's woman, a blot of exotic ink smeared across the bland, disbelieving faces of his colleagues. Speck suspected that the reason he took such delight in grime and mess, in not responding to the fussy and as he perceived feminine conventions of cleanliness and order, was precisely because he believed that the stronger the signal he sent out, the stronger the feminine force he would attract, the more devotedly female, the more stringently and assiduously woman.

Nathaniel's mother had died of pneumonia when Nathaniel was only four, and he could barely remember her. His father told him it was because she was so exhausted from looking after him, flooding Nathaniel with vague and unrelenting guilt. Nathaniel had learned to deal with the silence in his own head, the complete emptiness whenever he tried to imagine his mother's voice, by creating a vision of perfect womanhood that would remain forever unattainable.

Nathaniel's father was a doctor, a quiet man who maintained a public life of care and concern, and a private life of excess, drinking and going after Nathaniel, whom he openly blamed for the loss of his wife. Nathaniel spent as much time as possible out of the way, studying in his room, or experimenting with Bunsen burners and tungsten tubes in the dank safety of the basement.

The mail-order catalogue arrived express mail just as Speck came in sweating and panting from digging several eight-foot holes in his back garden. Speck didn't pause – he didn't wash or clear the glistening beads from his forehead and his back, he didn't take off his shoes or scrape the mud from his clothes – as he began to turn the pristine pages over with his thumb, his muddied thumb, and slowly the Orange Blossom girls were blackened and smudged, gummed up with clay and the earthy sweat of a North American man, a big man, a serious man, a man deeply flustered by their enticing faces, their glossy-lipped mouths. Finally, his thumb stopped. There she was, his Princess, his earnest woman set to wash his sea-stained rainment: Rashida. Maiden of India. For correspondence leading to marriage.

In truth, it wasn't her brown, velvety eyes peering over the grimy rim of his thumbnail that made him so sure, or the succulent coffee colour of her skin. It was that word: correspondence. Yes yes yes! Correspondence, which would lead to marriage! Such a practical theory! None of this murky business of dating and flowers, of overpriced dinners and diamonds, the whole messy artificial edifice of ridiculous illusions. A woman of words. No misunderstandings – just the pure lines of the alphabet on sheets of white vellum. And Speck knew that here he would shine, quoting from his colossal collection of books, from obscure texts and out-of-print sources – he knew he had what it took to make it from correspondence, the word cheering his heart anew, from correspondence, to marriage.

Make Thy Bed and Sleep in It

"There is hardly a sanctuary more noble and uplifting than the private sanctuary of one's bed. In fact, I regard it as a sacred place, muffled with sheets and blankets, filled with the aura of those who sleep and who dream there. It should never fall prey to the scrutiny of those not intimately associated with it, for it is the last place society itself has not intruded upon, a place of refuge from the bustling madness of our modern world. Cover up thy bed, all its excesses and personal vicissitudes, and remain true to its premise. No one can take that away from you, and that is surely a comfort in these stressful times."

From *Everyman's Guide to the Modern Universe and Household Management,* Nathaniel P. Speck, Professor of Medieval History, St Simons University, Chisholm, Nova Scotia

Three

Laura awoke with a start, realizing by the light streaming through the window that the alarm had failed to go off. She tried to focus her eyes on the clock. She could hear the boys downstairs shaking out cereal boxes, and the fridge door opening and closing. As she listened to the shower running in the bathroom she felt different, uneasy, as if she had dreamed something unsettling and it was still there. She crawled slowly out of bed and reached for her robe, draped across a chair where she had flung it last night, exhausted from a day with the boys. Gazing over at the bed she had just left, an idea crept up on her. It crept so slowly, so surprisingly, and yet so obviously, Laura could hardly believe she hadn't seen it before. A morning so like other mornings, its pattern so practised and familiar it was like breathing.

And yet there it was, staring her in the face. As it undoubtedly had been her entire married life.

Laura circled like a cat, peering, and mumbling to herself, and tilting her head this way and that. There it was, the whole bad mistake of it. Brian's side of the bed, unruffled, barely a fold or a crease, the corners gently tucked in and the seams all in their proper place.

But on the precarious other ground of the marriage bed, Laura's side, it was an entirely different affair. Everything was in disarray, folds and wrinkles rose up like mountains, the far corner of the sheet was twisted round and round on itself like a tornado. At the bottom of the bed, the sheet itself had been wrenched off the edge of the mattress, and half the blankets were on the floor.

Disparity of sheets!

The potent truth of what she had uncovered was so graphic she almost had to stifle a laugh at its sheer metaphorical genius. All those years she had been scratching around trying to figure out what would make their marriage better, what was wrong with it, whatever was the secret she couldn't quite uncover? She'd tried all the books, the recipes, the remedies, the theories, the silk lingerie, tried swallowing her anger, letting it go, following the precise formats of successful fighting, acquiescing to her husband on every point, standing her ground. But here it was, as literal as a toenail, why it never worked. Their personalities were miles apart, totally unsuited, oil and water.

Of course! Her excitement made him nervous, his placidity made her uncomfortable. She was passionate about the silent frozen world of her frogs, the cloistered calm of the laboratory, the presentation of a paper in a hushed room. He added up figures and put starch in shirts. All those years of struggling, trying to find a common ground, when everything was clear from their sleeping patterns.

Being a researcher, Laura knew she had to check out her hypothesis with someone else. But who did she know well enough to approach on this one? It wasn't like sneaking up on frogs, their breathing and heartbeats ground to a near halt. This would involve invading someone's bedroom in the early hours of the morning, couples still fuzzy from sleep, all those musty nighttime smells still lingering on the sheets, tell-tale stains dried like mysterious cloud formations.

It was then that the idea came to her, and a slow smile crept over her face, a smile totally unlike the one that had been frozen in place from the moment she said "I do." Forget about hibernation, cryopreservation, and the freeze tolerance of the North American wood frog. What Laura had in mind was business, and just as her husband came back into the bedroom, she saw the sign before her eyes:

> Twisted Inc.
> In-Depth Sheet Analysis for Couples in Trouble
> Confidential, Fast, Accurate
> Laura MacDonald, Bachelor of Science

The Bachelor of Science was the final stroke of genius, the hook that would establish her legitimacy to the wearied citizens of Chisholm, all those tired couples tramping about from day to day trying to figure out what was wrong with their relationships. Why the counselling never worked and the sap of love was dripping out of them year after year, slowly, painfully, inevitably.

"Wakey, wakey Laura, University Women's Breakfast this morning, remember?"

Laura winced. The University Women's Breakfast was a monthly obligation she abhorred, but which she took part in faithfully all the same.

"Wakey wakey yourself."

Brian looked over at his wife and raised his eyebrows.

"Well, aren't we in a snippy mood this morning."

"Au contraire," Laura replied, and began an amiable but tuneless whistling to herself, "I've never felt better."

And then she began selecting the appropriate clothing, sifting through the racks of her closet – a navy suit with brass buttons, tan linen slacks and a matching tan cotton sweater, nothing garish or extreme. She brushed her straight blond hair and took a look in the mirror. Laura MacDonald, Bachelor of Science. Laura MacDonald, Entrepreneur. Laura MacDonald, Twisted.

The University Women's Breakfast was, as far as Laura used to be concerned, as odious as the annual lobster boil, but she now recognized it as a marketing opportunity. It was held in the Faculty Lounge, its beige blend of scratchy polyester-covered chairs and fold-up card tables as conducive to lounging as a bed of nails. For the women's breakfast they dolled it up, of course, with white linens and fresh flowers, but there was no mistaking its tacky heart, though the women dressed up in their best and the room bore the sickly smell of mingled perfumes pulled from the backs of medicine closets for the event, and even the faculty lounge chef tried, apple-filled pancakes with whipped cream, or deep-fried smelts on one memorable, but less than successful morning.

Laura managed to enter the room without causing a single head to turn, the invisible domain of the plain, but she lifted her chin and strode in regardless, confident she could find some clients here among the faculty wives, the women who had been plucked here from otherwise successful lives elsewhere. That's what most of the talk was about – former lives, and so there was a good deal of wistful gazing out the window, as if gazing could bring it all back, and the effect of so many memories piled on each other gave the whole breakfast a sad, tired air. Laura could usually barely remember who was who, so she had them sorted in her mind based on what their husbands did: wife of biology, wife of physics, wife of psychology 101. There were also some former grads who came along, women like herself, the women who couldn't leave the university promise behind them, the women for whom the university breakfast was a welcome opportunity to get away from the kids and the housework and the unsettling quiet of an empty house at noon.

Into this strange intermingling of lost, unfinished, and unfulfilled lives came Laura reborn, who now sustained a tiny thrill even as she poured the weak coffee from the silver urn and turned to scan the crowd for prospects. She knew all the rumours about marriages that weren't working, but she couldn't let on. She would need to be subtle, clever, waiting for a weak moment to plunge in. As she considered this, a woman appeared at her elbow as if by magic, and began talking.

"Laura, hello, my name is Susan Barrett. Business, 1978. We met at the president's dinner last year?"

Laura turned to face the earnest expression behind the question mark, and tried to find something to remember this plain, brown-haired woman by. But there was nothing.

"Yes, yes, of course. How are you?"

"Well, I'm fine, really. I haven't been to one of these breakfasts for a while now, and I don't really recognize anyone."

"Susan, you said your name was again? Sorry, I'm hopeless at names."

"Yes, my husband runs the theatre down on Main. I'm sure you've been there from time to time!"

"Of course! Wife of *Rambo*!"

Susan laughed, fortunately possessing a sense of humour.

"I've tried, you know, I've tried to get him to bring in something else. Maybe a foreign film or two, a chick flick!"

"A chick flick in Chisholm! Now that would be something."

After some more chat, Laura beckoned Susan to a table by the window.

"Susan, you know you and I seem to hit it off, seem to have some kind of connection, wouldn't you say?'

Susan's face brightened.

"Well, yes, I guess I'd have to say yes."

"Now what about your husband? What did you say his name was?"

"Henry Thaddeus Barrett."

"Right, now what about the two of you? Did you guys hit it off right away?"

Laura was counting down for the kill.

"Well you know it's hard to say. Our families grew up together. We knew each other when we were five, for God's sake." Susan giggled. The caffeine was loosening her tongue. "Then one summer he kissed me and it all changed."

Talking to Susan was like talking to a teenager, but Laura couldn't fail to be impressed by the fact that Susan actually appeared to still be in love with her husband, still gushing and blushing over the first kiss.

"So what about you, Laura, you're married to one of the pillars of the community, now that must be exciting!" Susan's eyes sparkled with what she imagined to be the heady life of marriage to Brian MacDonald, pillar, etc.

It was a tense moment. She wondered how she could compress a lifetime of disillusionment into a single phrase that would neither scare Susan away, nor put her off the theory of the sheets. She remembered how Brian had courted her, back in their student days. He'd asked her if she'd wanted to go and see the autumn leaves, and she'd thought he meant on foot, but then he'd whisked her off in a rented Cessna, and they viewed the foliage from the air. It should have been wonderful but it was a colossal disappointment. Brian kept pointing out the controls, and how the plane worked, when all Laura wanted to do was to be mesmerized by the splash of colour moving below them. As she thought about it, she realized that was how their marriage had turned, everything important viewed from an enormous distance, the reality of who they actually were lost in the blur of day-to-day life.

"Mush, it's all mush."

"Excuse me?"

"Oh, sorry, I mean, blush, it makes me blush thinking about it."

"About what?"

Laura was on the point of losing her client. Time to smarten up.

"Have you heard about this new form of analysis?"

Susan fidgeted in her chair and shook her head.

"Well, it's brand new really, although when you think about it, it's as old as the hills. It's called sheet analysis."

"It's called what?"

"It has to do with sleep patterns. There's so much we can discover from a person by the way they sleep, and all the proof is right there, every morning, in the patterns the sheets make."

Susan didn't know whether she should laugh, or take it seriously. After all, Laura was a scientist, and the last thing she wanted to do was to look stupid in front of her, so she decided to take an interest.

"Who does this, sheet analysis?"

Laura smiled a broad and almost roguish smile.

"As a matter of fact, I do."

"Really? You?"

"Now I don't have my business cards made up yet, but if you like, I could head over to your house tomorrow morning, and do an on-site analysis."

Somehow Susan had managed to become Laura's first client, even though there were no problems in their marriage that she could see, and she hadn't even quite realized she had signed on. But now that she had...

"You know, I rushed out of the house in such a hurry this morning I didn't even have time to make the bed, so we could go over there right now, if you have the time."

If she had the time, now that was a laugh. Laura grabbed her purse, a notebook, and Susan's arm.

"Let's go!"

Susan and Henry's house was a plain little two storey built on a plain little street two minutes from the university, just around the corner from Laura and Brian's. It was a highly practical house, with lots of bedrooms, and toys in every room, and a big eat-in kitchen with a fake marble-top table. It smelled faintly of diapers, and talcum powder, and something which reminded Laura of Dettol. As they mounted the stairs Laura saw piles of clothes and laundry in a hill at the top, tiny balled-up socks and laughable sized underwear poking out from jeans and sweat shirts, a strap from a worn and weary looking grey bra hanging down from the top. Susan led Laura to their bedroom, and opened the curtains. There wasn't much in it – a couple of old dresser chests, a mattress with no headboard, another overflowing basket of laundry. They both stared down at the bed, as if waiting for the bed itself to speak. Then Laura took decisive action. She rolled back the blanket, hastily pulled up as Susan was leaving, to reveal the sheets beneath.

"Just as I thought!"

Susan gasped.

"Just look at that. I knew it."

They both stared down at the pale blue sheets, tucked primly into the corners of the mattress, scarcely a wrinkle to be found on either side. The whole dreamy flat expanse of it looked so inviting, Laura had to resist lying down on it, breathing in the cool seductive air of quiet sleep, no secrets, no tugging, pulling, or fretting.

"You two were made for each other. Look, it's all there!"

Susan breathed a sigh of relief, not that she was surprised. But maybe there was something to this. She couldn't help but notice that there was something terribly intimate about where you slept, something that couldn't be hidden by clever wit or self-denial. She decided to tell her sister Muriel about the service, Muriel who was always complaining that her husband was up to no good.

"What did you say your company was called?"

"Twisted."

"Give me your number."

And so Twisted Inc. took off. Laura found herself in bedrooms throughout Chisholm, peering, inspecting, circling, muttering appropriately timed ah has, and uh huhs, to add to the drama and general effect. Her system got more and more detailed, as she spoke with more and more wives (always wives, so it seemed), and examined the details of more and more sheets. Her notebooks began to look like this:

– Sheet pulled off mattress, far left. Instability of affection. Likely to stray.
– Sheet pulled off mattress, far right. A taste for violence, power, control.
– Wrinkles in a vertical pattern. Keeps everything in, hidden desires.
– Wrinkles in a horizontal pattern. A love of luxury.
– Wrinkles everywhere. Wants love, can't seem to hang on to it.
– Twisted sheet corners. No love ever enough.

Soon her analysis extended to pillows as well.

– Bunched up pillow. Intellectual frustration.
– Pillow pushed off bed. Stomach problems.

At first, Laura had been able to do the work of Twisted Inc. without saying anything to her husband, but she knew it wouldn't last. The business was growing in leaps and bounds, and Twisted had given Laura a kind of trumped-up bravado. She decided to tackle the whole subject of her new-found business at the annual Investors Club Dinner.

Sitting at the head table used to give her a kind of adolescent thrill, up there next to the Dean of the University, perched between the heads of companies and benefactors and assorted big shots. But it didn't take long for the thrill to abate, for the monotonous nature of the conversations to pall, and to recognize in one hideous flash of insight that no one cared about her except in terms of her relationship to the Dean.

But tonight she held a secret. In fact, many secrets. Gazing out at the assembled before her, she realized she had something on almost all of them. Their vices and predilections were as known to her as if they were wearing tee-shirts with the truth printed all over them. If she closed her eyes halfway she could imagine it, and from the sea of imaginary tee-shirts the letters disconnected and rose up as if they were floating in liquid, hanging like flags above the heads of their wearers:

- emotional detachment
- intellectual fraud
- laziness
- adultery
- boredom
- inability to satisfy.

Suddenly the reverie was shattered as the clinking of a spoon on a glass got everyone's attention.

"Ladies and gentlemen, welcome to this year's Investors Club Dinner."

Brian was standing so close beside her, she could almost smell the dry-cleaned wool of his trousers. On his seat there were a few stray crumbs from his dinner roll. Laura struggled to pay attention to what he was saying, or at least to appear to. She poked holes and made faces in her roll to keep herself amused.

"I have a few important announcements to make."

Brian droned on and Laura waited.

People stood up and took bows, distinctions were awarded for community service, Laura took more wine every time the busboy went by. Finally Brian sat down.

"Dearest, I've got something to tell you."

Brian looked alarmed. Why was she springing something on him here?

"You're not, are you? We've already got two."

Laura rolled her eyes.

"No, of course not. You had a vasectomy, remember?"

"Ssh, not so loud. Do you want everyone to hear?"

Just then the Bishop of Chisholm turned to them and put his arthritic finger to his lips. Laura realized someone was talking, the President of the University actually.

She waited for him to finish and sit down too, and then she turned her wine-flushed face towards her husband.

"I've started my own business."

Brian looked down at her, the way you would a gnat, or some other annoyance.

"What is it, Avon or something?"

"Tss. Avon." Laura turned her head away. "God."

"God then. What is it, Bibles?"

Brian chuckled at his own joke, and turned away. He had little interest in the activities of his wife. Laura was well aware of this, and so she practically shouted.

"I know who's fucking who in this town and people are paying me to find out!"

There was an abrupt silence. The murmur of polite chitter chatter went completely dead. Laura realized she'd have to do a little rapid damage control. It was, after all, confidentiality that made her business so successful.

"It's a line, a line from a new play." Laura stood up. "I saw it in Halifax, and I got so excited telling my husband here. Well, you'll all excuse me! It isn't often a play gets you right in the gut!"

Laura glanced over at Brian, who looked himself like he'd been punched in the gut, and smiled. She sat back down, and the murmuring began again, with somewhat renewed enthusiasm.

"What the hell was that?"

Laura paused for a moment before she replied. She had to admit this was the most animated conversation she'd had with her husband since she'd accidentally destroyed his hard drive with a virus while doing frog research.

"What I said. A business. It's called Twisted."

"Twisted." Brian replied, in a flat, dull voice.

"Oh never mind."

Brian decided his wife had simply had too much to drink, and that the best thing to do would be to ignore her and carry on. Sort of like their marriage. And besides, he had to address the issue of the grasshoppers. Everyone was expecting it. He stood up again and looked out at the crowds.

"Now, I know many of you have been dealing with the problem of grasshopper infestation."

There was a collective murmur that rose through the crowd, and more than a few heads bobbed up and down.

"As you know, the drought conditions made it a perfect breeding ground for them. As many as 25 to 30 hoppers a square yard have turned our crops into a joke. But..." Here Brian paused for effect. "But, there is good news from the weather experts in Halifax."

The murmur in the crowd had now risen to more of a din, and people were frowning and scratching their chins, looking apprehensive. They had been expecting some kind of announcement of financial compensation, and now they were going to get a weather forecast. Laura fidgeted in her seat, sensing the hostility that was gathering before her eyes.

"I've been on the blower with the Chief of Meteorology at Dalhousie." Laura hated it when Brian used words like "blower," as if the choice of friendly, local words would make up for the fact that there was no money coming.

"They're predicting a sudden drop in temperature within two weeks – a huge storm, a freak of nature, as it were. Ladies and gentlemen, Mother Nature is going to do our work for us and kill them off! You've got nothing to worry about!"

The room went eerily quiet. Brian straightened his tie and looked around at the faces of his clients, his colleagues, his friends and neighbours. His bluster seemed to have vanished, and in a small voice he asked if there were any questions.

"Too fucking right I got a question. In two weeks, I'm likely to be bankrupt! What the hell are you going to do about that?"

Although Brian was only an investment counsellor, and neither the head of the bank nor a representative of local government, he had come to represent authority in Chisholm, partly because his family went back so far. His father had been a founding member of the local Chamber of Commerce, and he was, after all, a financial success himself.

"There's absolutely nothing I can do about it, Cameron, and you know it. Now I'd ask you to watch your language, there are ladies present here, and try to look on the bright side of things. No eggs will hatch, not a single one."

Another voice sprang up from the crowd, a large woman in a pink dress.

"So, first the hoppers eat everything, then we get the cold to finish off our crop. Wow, I'm really thankful."

"Sally, I know how you feel. But we've got to stick together on this. It won't help if we're all warring with each other."

Laura could sense the explosive mix of fear and despair that was stirring itself up the more Brian spoke, and the more reasonable he sounded. She decided to get up and take matters in hand.

"Look, I know how you feel too, we're all neighbours here." Suddenly Laura had everyone's attention. "But I want you to know that Brian will be meeting with the Mayor just as soon as he can and work something out for you."

Laura could feel Brian tugging at the back of her jacket, trying to get her to sit down, and as she well knew, shut up.

"You know a MacDonald would never let you down!!"

A violent yank brought Laura down to her seat and Brian glared at her.

"I've just saved your ass out there!" Laura hissed. "You could at least be grateful!"

"I'm not going to see the Mayor."

"The hell you're not."

But by now Laura could see a few people watching them too closely, and she decided that for the sake of her business, and her husband, they should leave politely, and leave now. She stood up, a little shakily, and smiled, the purest smile she could muster, as she took Brian's arm and looked into his face. And there, staring down at her, staring in fact right through her clothes to the softest and most secret parts of her skin, was a look of wanting and lusting so intense, she staggered from the glare of it. Unfortunately, the feeling wasn't mutual.

Patience and Moderation in All Things

"*Haste is not prudent, dear men, in any endeavour. To take one's time is a sign of manhood, a sign of strength and wisdom. Rushing about, hither and thither, making silly mistakes, stumbling headlong into relationships, tsk tsk, this is no way to behave. From calm and considered action erupts the most fruitful result. To see oneself, one has to slow down. To see oneself, is next to godliness. Take your time, crack open the shell of your life with patience and moderation. The alternative is despair and the vast desert of lost opportunities that characterizes the twenty-first century.*"

From *Everyman's Guide to the Modern Universe and Household Management,* Nathaniel P. Speck, Professor of Medieval History, St Simons University, Chisholm, Nova Scotia

Four

The day of the lobster boil had been unnaturally bright, a sign that Speck should have paid attention to, and didn't. The sun rose and shone with a kind of microscopic fervour, pouring its unblinking light all over St Simons like an interrogation. And if it were possible to say that the sun shone more brightly on one house than any other, it would have to be on Speck's house, where Nathaniel rose and then fell back on the bed, his heart full of tumult at the thought that tomorrow, his new mail-order bride-to-be would be arriving from India, and his whole life would unfold before him, anew.

Speck took the opportunity to embrace his old disorderly ways for possibly the last time. He wore the same shirt he'd slept in, comfortably wrinkled and clinging, vaguely smelling of sweat and the breath mints he'd crushed in his pocket while sleeping, and he didn't bother to shave. He whistled to himself as he pulled on his gardening jeans, justifying it all by remembering what a mess he'd made of himself at last year's lobster boil. He went to the kitchen and heated up yesterday's chicory brew in the microwave, then cast a glance in the direction of the letters he'd been receiving from Rashida, piled up now in an old orange crate but which Speck intended to organize and relocate to a hand-carved wooden box he'd been making in the basement. Savouring his maleness for a while, he surrendered to a loud booming fart as he surveyed his domain from his full height – six foot four, and round as a giant gourd.

When Speck arrived at St. Simons that afternoon, he went straight to the main gymnasium to see what preparations were under way for the lobster boil. More than one hundred collapsible card tables had been set up across the floor, and each one was covered in a white tablecloth, bleached and starched pure of last year's excesses. Each table had four chairs assembled around it, and at the head of the room was a long row of rectangular tables, also covered in white cloth. There was no evidence of what was to come.

Various platters and bowls were set out along the long row of tables, and spoons and forks, and lobster crackers and metallic implements that looked like dental tools (or other forms of torture), and at the very end of the row was a huge metal pot, freestanding, which was to be the last place of rest for hundreds of lobsters now inching their way to their deaths in traps set out by St Simons local fishermen.

It was positively peaceful.

You might say that it looked like the set-up for a prayer meeting, an evangelical hubbub, a card game in the church basement, or some other such apparently wholesome endeavour. And in fact, although no one knew it then, some kind of conversion would take place there that night. It was whispering her name through the white cloths as they billowed in the slight breeze that skipped out under Nathaniel's feet, it was moving through the room like a snake, the hush hush of her name, if Speck had only been able to hear. Rashida, it circled the table legs like a ghost, Rashida, it lifted the hairs in Nathaniel's nose so that they tickled and he sneezed, and a young boy at the far end of the gym, who was fixing a broken table leg, looked up in surprise and then waved. Speck heard a jet moving overhead, and the distant sound of a piano from somewhere in the music department, but he couldn't hear the whisper of her name, and that was to be his downfall.

From the other end of the gymnasium, someone else was looking in. Tabitha's heart went out to the implied sense of order suggested by the tidy arrangement of tables, each one a perfect white diamond against the backdrop of the oak gym floor. Tabitha liked to imagine what things would look like from the air – and here was something beautiful, a harlequin's garb, right here on the gym floor of St Simons, a transformation made possible by her imagination alone. (And the involuntary deaths of hundreds of innocent lobsters, she heard her mother's voice from the stratosphere). The harsh clacking of her mother's tongue made it almost impossible to hear the whisper jet of Rashida's name as it curled around Tabitha's feet like a cat, but she thought she heard something, and without knowing why, she stroked her hair, and felt a faint flush starting at her cheeks. Just then her dream was interrupted by the sound of Nathaniel's sneeze at the other end of the room, and she closed the door noisily and banged up the stairs to her office, suddenly in a foul mood.

No one really knows whether the high pitched wailings of lobsters as they are dunked alive into vats of boiling water are cries of torment or whether death hits instantly and the sound is simply a biological anomaly, but no one at the lobster boil that early summer night really cared. It was time for revelmaking, feasting, everyone letting their academic hairs down and going native, all those stiff-shirted academics from away. Brian was the first to arrive, because it was his job to cook the lobsters. He had been enlisted by the Dean. In fact, the whole boil had been his idea from the start. He saw it as a way of being "just one of the boys," a way of (literally) rolling up his sleeves and getting dirty. It was all so collegial, and not to mention a way of supporting the local fishermen. With the money they got from the annual boil, the fishermen got not only a good laugh but also some big steaks from the local Sobeys and a few renovations to appease the wife.

Laura never came to the boil, and for Brian, this was the only thorn in the whole affair. He was always embarrassed about it, especially since he had to make up excuses for her every year, and wasn't it a shame, everyone said, how she hadn't been able to make it to even one, and here it was going on for ten years. Last year he told everyone that Laura had been bitten by a raccoon and that she'd had to have a rabies shot, which was none too pleasant. This year he decided to tell them that she'd developed temporary agoraphobia. The truth was that she couldn't stand to see her husband plunging the lobsters into their steaming deaths with such relish, nor could she stand to see the sickening smile of victory that swept over his face as he pulled them out again, all pink and powerless, their claws useless. She'd stood at the back of the room, at the very first boil, and seen him do it. She'd left again quietly, before anyone knew she had been there, and she'd taken her stand. There wasn't a lot she could do, but this was something. Laura sharpened the thorn a little with every passing year, as Brian's embarrassment, highly public, accumulated.

By the time Tabitha arrived, many of the tables had been filled, and the room itself was crammed with voices. She waved to Brian by the lobster vat, and he waved back, noting with interest that from a distance he could make out the silhouette of a black push-up bra beneath her prim white shirt. A small lobster dropped from his hands and scuttled over the edge of the table, but he recovered his composure fast enough to catch it and drop it into the vat. Tabitha searched the room for some familiar faces, but everyone seemed to be turning away from her and towards someone else. Finally she saw a table that appeared to have one or two vacant seats, and she walked over. She looked back at Brian. She pictured his hands, raw and vaguely salty from handling the lobsters, snapping open the front closure of her bra and her breasts tumbling out, filling his hands, the salt sea sweetness of the lobster clinging to everything. For a moment the image clouded over her brain; she saw her breasts spilling and tumbling over and over again, the bras coming on and off with alarming speed, like the pages of one of those books you flip rapidly with your thumb to create a moving picture effect. She laid her hands on the back of one of the chairs to steady herself and turned to face her table-mates. The first person her clear blue eyes rested on was Nathaniel Speck, who was busy calibrating the decibel level of the room's general din.

"Too loud for you?" she asked.

"Ah, Tabitha, what a pleasure. I didn't see you come in." He plopped his portable decibel meter back into his front right pocket and straightened up in front of Tabitha. "I just bring this along to give me something to do at these awful functions."

It was always a surprise to hear Nathaniel speak. His voice was resonant and dark, almost elegant, and it came as a slight shock, because of its source. Everyone knew that Nathaniel was a genius, a brilliant scholar in the medieval field, no one doubted that. Everyone knew how subtle and ingenious and clever his papers were, and they were published everywhere, and in many languages. His *Everyman's Guide to the Modern Universe and Household Management* had become a runaway success, containing as it did pompous but completely uninformed slugs of wisdom to guide the man of the twenty-first century through the tangled forests of contemporary relationships and household challenges. But if you saw him on the street you'd have been tugging in your pocket for change. His hair was so matted together with dirt and grime it took on new kinds of properties; it wasn't really like hair at all, it was more like some sort of fibrous insulating material. "Tabitha?"

"Nathaniel, I'm terribly sorry. What were you saying?" She began straightening out the folds in her jacket and clearing her throat.

"Nothing important. Can I get you a drink?" Nathaniel was being positively gallant tonight.

"What is that you've got, local plonk?"

"I'm afraid so."

"Okay, thanks." She didn't want any at all, but she needed a few moments to pull herself together. She watched Nathaniel striding back across the room with two glasses of what appeared to be red wine, the wine sloshing about in the glasses and staining what was already a shirt full of stains. She watched as he got closer and closer, and put the glass out in front of her, now half empty.

"Bottoms up, Nathaniel." She raised the glass to her lips, and smiled. "Bottoms up."

The talk that followed was mostly about research grants — who got one, who didn't, who should have, who shouldn't, who had the longest single title (not counting colons). It was amiable, and a few others joined in, although many people took a wide berth around Tabitha and Speck, oddballs even by St Simons standards. Soon it was time for the food to begin. A few people brought their own lobster crackers, and other implements, scoops and gougers, a personal array. Speck himself had fashioned his own set from some old dental tools he'd picked up at a garage sale, and he brought them out and displayed them proudly on a bed of red velvet, which he set down next to the pile of disposable plastic bibs that were found on every table. Smiling and unnaturally red lobsters were dancing all over the bibs, a statement whose irony obviously went unnoticed by the manager of Sobeys, who had donated them. Tabitha always hated wearing the bibs, a return to some sort of babyhood, although it made her think more of getting old and drooling over her Jell-O.

She made her way to the food table, picked up her plastic plate and began filling it with coleslaw and potato salad, two things which she never ate except at university functions. A large pool of grease had formed under one of the glass bowls where someone had stood too long in conversation while their spoon dripped. Tabitha began looking at it for signs, omens, portents of things to come. If tea leaves, why not mayonnaise, she reasoned. But she read nothing, only the tedium of the gathering itself, the way her life spread out like the grease spot, sinking, sinking, sinking deeper into the fabric of oblivion. There had to be something else, and it was going to be the phalanx. For a moment she imagined she could see the tracings of buildings and blueprints in the stained pool before her. She felt a flicker of excitement when Brian plopped a bright red plump lobster on her plate and she caught sight of his arms, where the sleeves had been rolled up, and the hair was suggestively dark and fine. But she knew these were just temporary distractions, and she knew it now even before anything got started. Perhaps it was simply the natural consequence of getting older – fewer sustaining delusions.

Once back at her table, she began cracking open her lobster the way she had been taught. First she cracked off the claws and the tail. Then, from the small end of the body she pushed the largest piece of meat with her spoon until it was forced out the other end. She dipped it in a puddle of butter on her plate and took the first bite. It was always heavenly, that first sweet taste, and for a moment she forgot where she was and who she was sharing her table with. Nathaniel was already on his second lobster. Small mountains of shell and discarded bits of lobster were forming on tables throughout the gymnasium, and the din of crackers cracking and lobsters being torn apart was like the sound of bones breaking or forks being scraped across a china dish. Lobster shells flew everywhere, and people had bits on their fingers, in their hair, on their clothes, butter dripped from their chins and the really committed were sucking stringy tender morsels right out of the claws like straws.

Debauched didn't really describe it, although it came close. Nearly two hundred people enjoying themselves tearing out the insides of some unfortunate shellfish boiled alive in a vat. Nathaniel was in the ecstatic thick of it. He was now on his third lobster. His beard was sticky with lobster roe and bits of shell and grease, a kind of gruesome fishnet. He wore plastic swim goggles to prevent any flying shell from going into his eyes, and he didn't even bother with the bib, there was so much lobster spattering from his teeth. Nathaniel loved the lobster boil. He loved it so much he had forgotten to double-check the date of the plane ticket he had sent to Rashida. He thought it was tomorrow. He had planned everything smug in that knowledge. He saw the lobster boil as a kind of last rite, the ritual feasting before the purge. This thought gave him extra gusto as he tore off a huge claw and picked up his pliers. He was just about to crack it open when a scream shot through the room. A weird pause followed, as a few lobsters thudded down on plates and the clickety clack of lobster paraphernalia dropping from people's hands collapsed the silence for a few moments. Everyone had stopped and turned to look at the woman who stood in the doorway, a woman in deep turquoise silk with a golden scarf over her head, her hands raised up to her open mouth. No one knew who she was. Except Nathaniel, who knew immediately, and stood up from the table and called out her name, hopeless as he knew the gesture was, and yet powerless to stop himself. In a panic he began to run towards her, a mistake he realized as soon as he put one foot in front of the other. At the sight of this huge goggled man, puffing and sweating and covered in white greasy flesh from head to toe, she turned and fled. Nathaniel found out later that she had gone straight back to the airport and boarded the next available flight, horrified by the spectre of her future husband lumbering towards her like a madman, smeared with lobster guts.

Nathaniel was not to be consoled. In fact, he went back to his table and wept, openly, gushingly, endlessly. People started picking up their lobster implements again and the hum of talk began to rise like a small sea of flies throughout the room. Tabitha was stunned into silence. Nathaniel snorted into his napkin and Tabitha watched him for a while, dumbstruck, at the dreadful outpouring of emotion that had become Nathaniel Speck. She handed him his wine but he waved it away. Slowly the tears began to subside and Tabitha led him up from his chair and out of the hall, avoiding the eyes of the Dean and all the assembled there, who watched in amazement as Nathaniel left like a condemned prisoner, softly, weeping into his hands.

She didn't really know why she did it, but she placed him gently in her car and drove him home. She didn't ask any questions. He offered no response, except to point her in the right direction as they headed out of the university and down the main street. From the back, it might have looked as if she were driving a bear home, a wounded animal. Nathaniel's house was just out of town, on a small, quilted hillside that looked out over Bluejacket Bay. In fact, his house was right beside her property – the future Harmony! Nathaniel's house was one of the oldest in the area, although not decrepit, because although he had no notion at all about interior design or household cleanliness, he was a good workman, and everything had been tightened, fixed or restored somehow, so that the walls were sturdy and watertight, the roof was sound, and the windows hermetically sealed. Tabitha had never been inside, but she waited at the door as Nathaniel fumbled to locate his keys and the decibel meter fell from his pocket sending out a little beeping sound into the night. It didn't seem right to go yet, she reasoned. Perhaps she'd make him a cup of tea.

Once inside, Tabitha switched on a few lights and took in the view. From the large front window you could just make out the lights of fishing boats in the bay, and each time a car went by on the road below a sweep of additional light would wash over the front room, which looked as if someone were either moving in or moving out. There were boxes of books stacked about, empty cans of paint and jars of chemicals, several broken bits of furniture. A pile of what appeared to be clothes or old rags was spilling from a green garbage bag in the corner, and brooms and mops and buckets filled with cleaning supplies, apparently newly bought, sat near the door. Nathaniel appeared to be on the point of collapse, leaning against the wall, his pale face puffed and swollen from crying, so Tabitha steered him down the corridor to the right, assuming that somewhere down the gloomy hallway there would be a bed and a warm blanket. There was. She patted the bed and he climbed in, like a small, obedient child. She pulled some sort of ratty musty-smelling afghan over him and walked quietly out of the room, towards where she imagined the kitchen would be.

As she flicked on the light in the kitchen, she wondered for a moment what the hell she was doing there. The kitchen itself was spotless. It must have been first on Nathaniel's list of clean-up projects. Everything was put away; in the cupboards all the jars had been marked – rice flour, brown sugar, Thompson's raisins – in a neat and perfectly even hand. The sink shone like a mirror and the stove glistened. Tabitha found a box of Twinings Earl Grey tea and a cup, cracked but immaculate, near the kettle. She set the kettle on the stove and waited for it to boil. Next to the general mess and grime of the rest of the house the kitchen was a kind of oasis, and Tabitha huddled there, on a rocking chair set near the window and a curious kind of calm settled over her. The kind of calm that comes when you lie down for a rest in the afternoon, and there's nothing for you to do, and no one will come and bother you, and the pillow under your head is plump and cool and soft and a slight breeze lifts the curtains at the window beside your bed. You could just drop off to sleep and lie there forever, frozen in a dream.

The whistling of the kettle made Tabitha jump, and she got up so fast the rocking chair tipped backward and fell over, knocking a thick wad of pale yellow sheets of paper off a pile of boxes stacked up behind it. The kettle whistled and steamed but it seemed more important to pick up the papers and try to put them back in order. Someone had tied a velvet string around the sheets like a belt but most of them had spilled out anyway and Tabitha recognized the script on them from the labelled jars in the kitchen. "Dearest Rashida" the first one began, and Tabitha knew she should put them back immediately and turn the kettle off and go. Instead, she filled the cracked cup with boiling water, put the teabag in and inhaled the fragrant smell of bergamot oil, stood the rocker back in its place, checked to make sure that Nathaniel was sleeping soundly, and settled in for a read. Beside her the blackened window (not yet cleaned) revealed nothing, not even the dawn as it rose a velvety pink beyond its greased and grimy frame. And as the sun came up over the turbulent waters of Bluejacket Bay, Tabitha was still reading, the measured, careful, yet passionate correspondence of Nathaniel Speck, Mister Medieval, and his intended.

Correspondence – A Private Matter

"*Love letters should be written in confidence and read the same way. And love letters should remain discreet – do not go gushing forth about your heart and spilling your guts. Describe your hobbies! How you spend your days! But do not go on and on with a kind of love-crazed madness, for your words will appear contrived, false, overblown. There is joy in simple correspondence, between like-minded individuals who do not need the false crutch of excessive sentiment. Be so advised, oh writer.*"

From *Everyman's Guide to the Modern Universe and Household Management*, Nathaniel P. Speck, Professor of Medieval History, St Simons University, Chisholm, Nova Scotia

Five

Chosen and Most Beloved,

If you want to imagine heaven, picture a house that faces out to the sea. Couch grass curled over itself at the sea's edge and the smooth cold sea hearts of stones which I will press into your hands with my own. The salt-sea tingle of the wind in October, the crackle, warm and woodsy, of bark turning over in the fireplace of the house that faces out to the sea. A man who lives in that house and faces out, across the shoreline, across other seas, to where you are, chosen one, my intended.

I will turn my kingdom upside down for you, if you will it, beg like a dog, shed my tears in a silent cup. I will raise the roof to shout out your name, surround us with walls to be alone together. I will share my house, my sea, my every dream. I will crown your heart with the flowers of my love, and we will breathe the sweet fragrance of that union forever. My beloved one, I await your answer.

Dear Mr. Speck,

It is very kind of you to be writing. I am a tidy, outgoing person with lots of friends. This house sounds very pleasing. But I am not at all sure about this raising of the roof business. Please explain.

Dearest Intended,

Your words pierce me to the quick with their candour and their simplicity. My jewel, you are a rare and precious discovery. All that I have is yours, and all that I aspire to. There will be no greater match than ours.

I won't really raise the roof, dear heart, it's simply an expression of reverent joy, a kind of love-infested hoopla!! As you will see from the photograph I have enclosed, the roof is firmly, fixedly, finally attached, as you and I will be, dear one, heart's ease, as you and I will be, very soon. And please, do call me Nathaniel.

Dear Mr. Nathaniel,

Many thanks for your prompt reply. I am 5' 7", 120 lbs, with brown hair and brown eyes. I have six brothers and sisters. I hope to get job as secretary. My father and I like to listen to country music on the radio. Do you have a radio?

Most Cherished of Intended Ones,

Radios, televisions, microwaves...anything you want, oh beloved one!! You can fill the house with electronic gadgets, I will build you a shed to house them all, I will build a monument to them!! And I will replace the nasal twang of that music which now fills your ears, oh blissfully ecstatic radio waves who enter the delicate ears of my beloved each and every day, I will replace it with Mozart! With Bach! With Beethoven! Fear not the painful mediocrity of that music which now surrounds you – I will banish it forever!

Most beloved…a secretary? My fortune I bequeath you in perpetuity. There will be no need to pound those soft fingers on typewriter keys, to strain those cinnamon-coloured eyes in the glare of a computer screen. Kisses will flow from my lips to yours, money will flow from my pockets. Abundance, our motto, in all things. Dearest, put aside these petty longings. My kingdom awaits you.

Dear Mr. Nathaniel,

Please explain what means perpetuity.

Chosen and Most Beloved,

Forever, dearest.

Dear Mr. Nathaniel,

My father says he wasted the wages of one whole year to send me to school. Will you be sending the money to him also?

Dearest,

Perhaps this is the time my beloved to send you a sampling of my thoughts on finance in marriage. Dearheart, my entire estate I put before your bright eyes, to do with as you wish. Mistress of my house, of my heart, to you all coffers do flow. May you keep the house and dole out the dollars as you will, in good counsel, as I am sure you would, a goodly wife and all. Because in truth I do not care about money, and if you wish to buy a few chickens with it, that is fine, and if you wish to order silks with it, that is fine also, for we shall prosper regardless. To strengthen my suit, may

I offer you a sampling of what I now possess, or should I say, what you now possess, and what I consider to be of value:

28 pairs of pure wool socks
aluminum siding (impervious to wind)
several acres of wooded land
tenure.

Dearest, until our next correspondence.

Dear Mr. Nathaniel,

To strengthen your suit, my father says you need a good tailor. This is what my father is doing. Would you please explain exactly what means tenure?

Beloved and Most Adored,

Forever, dearest.

Tabitha read the letters until she could no longer keep her eyes open, through the luminous dark and into the dawn, with the compelling pleasure of stumbling across someone's secrets. It wasn't easy to reconcile the Nathaniel she thought she knew, the matted hair and the rumpled clothes, the sheer, bulky breadth of him, with the elegant romanticism of these letters, except for the voice. Nathaniel's voice! If you could have had sex with a voice, then Nathaniel's would have been a celebrity by now, a love-God of the vocal chords. But from whatever, locked-away, private place that heavenly voice came from, so too did the letters.

But there was no way this would have worked anyway, no way. She'd read Rashida's letters. She was too young! Too inexperienced! What did she want with an oafish forty-plus professor? Admittedly, one with a flair for words, but still. And what was he thinking? Beloved! Adored! Hah! What a load of garbage, she muttered to herself, even as she studied the letters. Stilted, archaic, ludicrous. The eroticism of those who stayed too long at school, she decided, ignoring her own, lifelong misunderstanding of love's language. She read on.

Dear Mr. Nathaniel,

The arrival of my ticket fills me with great joy. From the window of my father's house I see nothing but a field and an old donkey. Soon the donkey will be dead. Well, you know what it is I mean.

Oh Virtuous and Wise Woman,

Of course!! New life ahead! The donkey dies and Rashida lives! Of course, I trust you are not comparing me to the old donkey, hah hah. If I am forced to think of myself in this way at all, I prefer to see myself as an old lion, Still proud and, dare I say it, virile — regal king of the jungle!! Followed by a giant roar. ROAR! Until next time,
Your devoted old lion,
Nathaniel

Dear Mr. Nathaniel,

Your words fill me with confusion. What you were saying about the donkey and the lion. Proud and virile. What is this western claptrap, my father says. My mother weeps. My bags are packing all the while and I am still very excited about coming. If you are the lion, then perhaps I am the lamb. At least, that is what I said. And that is at the exact same moment the weeping started. Go figure, as I heard on the radio.

Dearest Lambikins,

Perhaps I was too bold in my last correspondence, carried away by the prospect of your arrival and all the silliness of love!

Love! I am humbled at your feet, in fact, it is I who must be the tender lamb, curled before you, and prepared to become all that you wish of me.
Yours fleecily,
Nathaniel

Dear Mr. Nathaniel,

It would be grateful if you could arrange to send some money. It might help family to get over the whole lion/donkey/lamb business.

Beloved of Beloveds, Chosen of the Chosen, Queen of My Heart,

Have I not explained that everything I have is yours? But I would prefer to wait until you are here, banks being what they are, foreign exchange, planes carrying money that drop from the sky, etcetera, etcetera, etcetera. Rest assured that you will want for nothing. (Except perhaps rest from me and my undying devotion!!)

Dear Mr. Nathaniel,

My father has asked me to write again, very sorry. He says there are many wireless ways of transferring money, and that no alarm is necessary.

Chosen One,

Is it your father's habit to read your mail? Surely not our private and loving correspondence, our most confidential of revelations and promises. Such indiscretion raises the alarm more than any petty money worries! Dearest, you must keep our letters to yourself, the innermost outpourings of our most private hearts. Tsk. Tsk. And loving kisses.
Your dearest Nathaniel.

Stabbed with a sudden pang of guilt, Tabitha put the letters down, stood up and peered out the front window. The sky was now a violent purple, a bruise from horizon to horizon, winter on its way. She pictured the grasshoppers, storming their way towards Chisholm, unaware of the chilly death that awaited them. From down the hall she could hear a fitful snoring, as if Nathaniel might be on the verge of waking up. She went back in the kitchen and tried to rearrange the letters the way they were before she had read through them, but they refused to stay in the neat little bundle as she had found them, and kept popping out from the sides of the ribbon, like stuffing. By now the snoring was rising to a massive gurgling growl, and Tabitha began to get nervous. She tried lining up the sheets and straightening the edges, but none of the sheets seemed to match up and the whole pile was becoming more disordered than ever. Finally she decided to just stuff the wad in the box and hope that Nathaniel wouldn't decide to look over them until enough time had passed that he wouldn't remember whether he had left them in that state or not. She closed the lid on the box, and sneaked quietly out the door.

The morning air was sharp and cold, a crisp hint of things to come. Tabitha wanted to take a short walk around her property, but she realized she had left her jacket back at the lobster boil. She got into her car and turned on the heat, full blast, but got nothing but a shower of dried leaves through the vents and a shot of frigid air. She sopped up the condensation with the one remaining Kleenex in her pocket, Nathaniel having gone through the rest on the drive home the night before, and headed down the hill towards home.

Beloved! Most precious! She could hardly believe the words. So outdated, so idiotic. A little warmth had begun escaping through the heater vents and Tabitha stopped shivering. It wasn't a long drive home, and there were very few cars on the road. Tabitha took the time to admire the square patches of land that spread out on either side of the road, the way they criss-crossed in patterns all the way down to the sea, then simply plunged off the cliffs to the Atlantic below. She saw the small wooden houses and cottages that characterized the landscape, small, white or yellow or blue ones, with two windows and a door at the front like a child's drawing of a house. Each one looked the same, except that they faced in different directions, as if they didn't want to be caught all looking the same way.

Forever! Dearest! What a load of crap that was, she thought, as she turned on to the road that led home. Heart's ease. Where had Nathaniel come up with that one? Must have been from some old manuscript, she decided, some moth-eaten, dog-eared, ancient relic. But still, she couldn't help but recognize in that lunatic gushing of rubbish a trace of desire she had experienced herself, once, anyway. As she turned into the driveway, closed off the heat, and slid out into the morning air, the shivers began anew. She knew it was the result of no sleep, as well as the morning chill. Heart's ease. What was that anyway? But try as she might to beat them off, the words clung, and she had to wash them away in a hot shower, before they hung around long enough to get comfortable.

Shielding Yourself from Silken Temptation

"Seduction comes in many forms, and may even greet you at your workplace, where you least expect it. Be forewarned! The quickie is the domain of the less than manly man. Put a closed sign over the doorway to your heart, and keep it chaste. Is there anything more frightening than the thought you could lose everything, on a whim? Be strong!! Be wary!"

From *Everyman's Guide to the Modern Universe and Household Management*, Nathaniel P. Speck, Professor of Medieval History, St Simons University, Chisholm, Nova Scotia

Six

By now Tabitha had undertaken every form of financial planning there was – and together with Brian had followed through on all possible scenarios, including early retirement, carrying on to the bitter end, real estate, stocks, shifting money here, stashing money there. But for all of Tabitha's hinting and suggestions – who would have thought there was such erotic subtext buried in the language of one's investment profile? – Brian didn't seem to have twigged to her seduction. During yet another consultation, Brian tried to get to the root of what it was she wanted from her portfolio.

"Now when do you wish to withdraw?"

"Oh, never, never." Tabitha murmured, inching closer to Brian on the couch. "I never want to withdraw."

Brian carried on as if he hadn't heard her.

"What kind of tolerance do you think you have for risk?"

Tabitha fluttered her eyelashes and looked heavenward.

"Enormous. Huge. I'd risk anything. "She placed her hand on Brian's thigh. "And you?"

Brian edged away.

"Oh me, I don't like risks. I like to play it safe. Now, let's see. What about your investment profile...conservative, or aggressive?"

The effort it took for Tabitha to resist growling and baring her teeth was considerable.

"Conservative, oh definitely, conservative."

"Good, good, now let's see what we can do here. Now, you're definitely going to want to take out some money at some point, despite what you said. Let's establish a personal financial goal and a time frame, shall we?"

While Brian droned on about RRSPs and RRIFs and stocks and bonds Tabitha began to realize another tack might be necessary.

That night, as Tabitha was putting together her course outlines, she finally had to admit to herself that seduction through financial planning was not working. In fact, Brian didn't seem to even know he was being seduced, and this somewhat compromised her theory that he was desperate to escape the clutches of the bourgeois family and become a happy libertine. Her slender fingers lay on the opened book in front of her: *The Utopian Vision of Charles Fourier*. Fourier had theorized that there were twelve fundamental passions, governed by the Law of Attraction, and surely Brian must have at least one! He did have two jobs – perhaps that was it! La Papillone! A natural desire for variety. But what she desperately wanted to share with someone, and for some bizarre reason she had chosen Brian to be that someone, was La Composite, the most beautiful passion of all. Though she had to admit the idea was virtually untranslatable into English, La Composite seemed to mean the combination of two or more passions, nourishment of the soul, the senses, the intellect. She would liberate Brian from the family structure that so stifled him, turning him inward, and set his path outward, to where the joys of community held open their embrace. Long Live La Composite!

When Fourier had first come into her life, back in graduate school, she'd had no idea he would change her whole outlook on the world. A friend had plopped his "Table of The Unproductive Classes of Civilization" across her desk, as a joke:

Domestic Parasites:
> Women: absorbed in household work
> Children: in a city, utterly useless
> Servants: superfluous workers in luxury trades

Social Parasites:
> Armies: young men wasting the best years of their lives
> Fiscal agents: useless administrative bodies
> Manufactures: producing poor quality goods, especially those undertaken for the government, which everyone conspires to defraud
> Commerce: how much is truthful?
> Transportation: following unnecessarily circuitous routes

Accessory Parasites:
> Unemployed: work must be made more attractive!
> Sophists: controversy muddles every subject; these are parasites who incite others into political intrigues and unproductive cabals
> Idlers: men of good breeding who spend their lives doing nothing
> Dropouts: people in open rebellion against work, laws, customs, and established practices, including those who run lotteries and gambling houses (true social poisons), adventurers, prostitutes, vagrants, beggars, pickpockets, brigands, etc.

"What do you think of those brigands, eh?" was the note scribbled across the bottom of the list, which had been photocopied from a book on Fourier wrongly shelved and discovered by her unsuspecting friend while researching the mating habits of ferrets. "Or those unproductive cabals!"

But Tabitha had recognized, in that orderly categorization of civilization and its follies, someone who understood her. Someone who believed that another way was possible. And as his books began to pile up by her bedside, he became more than just another subject for study, yet another human being addicted to the persistent idea that if only societies set up the right conditions, everything would work out the way it should. The more she studied his highly thought-out prescription for living, his mania for order and his endless lists, the more of a soulmate he and his ideas became.

Brian's father, William Donald MacDonald, also had a vision, and while having the very first dry-cleaning business in Chisholm was somewhat paltry next to the complete reworking of civilization, there was sort of a pattern, wasn't there? Not exactly Utopia, but a kind of synergistic connection, no? The idea set a plan in motion in Tabitha's mind, as she began listing the varieties and combinations of silk lingerie that she possessed, the delicate lace straps and removable parts, the sweet pinks and mauves of bras, panties, garters and camisoles which she would bring, breathless, to Brian for dry-cleaning. Still warm from her body, she would do her best to bring them, still scented with oils and perfumes. And she would place them in his hands, and then how would he cope? It's true that most people didn't dry-clean their underthings, but since when did Tabitha consider herself most people?

Tabitha headed out towards her back porch, where a cool evening breeze was making its way from the ocean across Chisholm Harbour and over the turrets and towers of St Simons, picking up the scent of ink and old books, of university romances begun in libraries and examination halls where long meaningful glances could be sustained like harvest moons over the scrape and shuffle of pencil on paper, frantic erasures and the hair-pulling, clock-watching heat of mid-terms. But Tabitha felt something else on the breeze too, something rank and familiar, a powdery presence which she recognized all too quickly.

Mother.

Tabitha watched as a single cloud in the darkening sky began to twist and form itself first into a mouth, and gradually into a face. She heard the voice like a rasping whisper.

"Tabitha! What do you think you're doing – seducing a man who seems perfectly happy."

Tabitha rolled her eyes. Perhaps it was some apparatus associated with guilt – the spirit of Rosa was always popping in, unannounced. Each time she did, Tabitha fumbled about in her brain for a way to say she was sorry, but Rosa always said something to annoy her, so closure never came, or forgiveness.

"Oh, you want him for a commune." The cloud tilted a little, and the mouth formed itself into a yawn. "By the way, a little soy in your salad dressing would perk it up."

Tabitha frowned and thought hard. "It's not a commune, why doesn't anybody get it? Besides, you should know better than anyone. Love is the domain of unreason. Fourier, nineteenth century. "

"It's not love, Tabitha, come on."

Tabitha suddenly shouted.

"Ma, where do you get off trying to give me advice on my life? Every man you hitched up with was a disaster."

"My point exactly."

"Well it doesn't mean I'm going to go the same way."

"They can all be seduced, you must know that. He's harder to get, that's all. Leave him alone."

Suddenly the cloud turned in on itself, the mouth disappeared down into a crevice, and the eyes flattened, detached and dissipated into the sky. Tabitha looked down the street to where she could see the lights at Brian and Laura's house shining into the night, lighting up the swing set and the tree house in their back yard. A dog was barking in the field and the tall purple lupins planted against the fence swayed moodily in the breeze.

A few more clouds appeared, pushing what was left of Rosa out of Tabitha's field of vision, intent on their own business. Tabitha wondered if everyone had their own cloud, their own annoying, nay-saying demons in the shadows. She shook her head, as if to clear out the cobwebs, went back inside, and began folding and listing her underwear.

She did it in alphabetical order, a habit she had begun as a child and never left behind. The softness of the underwear in her hands set off one memory, and then another, as if she was being swirled backwards down a silken time tunnel.

"All the dinosaurs that begin with D. Di...Di...Diplodocus. Dimetrodon. Deinonychus." The little girl rhymed off the dinosaurs like beads on a rosary, slowly settling into step with her thoughts, the multi-syllabic beasts flowing like a balm. "Dinosaurs beginning with E. More tricky. Echinodon. Edmontosaurus. Euoplocephalus." A door slammed below her room and she heard angry shouts. A steady stream of reptiles ticked across her brain in a demonic kind of order, their rhythms like a pulse somehow more natural, more comforting than her own heartbeat, which couldn't be trusted to remain steady, but which went off lurching and skipping and rising and falling, entirely on its own.

Tabitha hid in the corner of her room with her dolls – dolls with pink dresses and panties on the left, dolls without panties on the right, dolls who had lost a limb or two propped up in the middle by their stronger, more mobile sisters. She heard a heavy footstep on the stairs...

"All the stories that have animals in them. Goldilocks and the Three Bears. Little Red Hen..."

Another creak on the stairs.

"The Three Little Pigs. Cinderella..."

The last few steps mounted quickly, a quickening of the breath.

"The Frog Prince..."

And with that, the door burst open.

"How'zzz my little prinzess?" Rosa's first husband, fuzzy with gin, grabbed her arm and pulled her roughly towards him. "Wanna see what I have for you?"

The Ugly Duckling. The Ugly Duckling.

He pushed her away, and from his pocket he produced a blue and yellow striped whirligig, slightly dented, and which didn't really whirl, and a penny. She backed away towards where the bed met the wall, crawled up without turning her back to him, pulled a pillow close to her chest. The penny landed on the floor and a small puff of dried mud shook out, leaving a tiny dark aura around it.

"Don't I even get a thank you?" he shouted. Tabitha could hear her mother downstairs, sobbing. "Jesus."

Tabitha turned towards her dolls, curled her knees up to her chest, and mumbled thank you.

"I don't know why the hell your mother doesn't teach you any manners."

He raised his hand as if to hit her, changed his mind, and went off in search of Rosa. Tabitha picked up the whirligig and chucked it in the wastebasket, tut-tutting to her dolls as she did. Then she picked up the penny, and began scraping at the dirt with her thumb. Eventually a face began to emerge from the copper, the cameo of a distant queen, just about the size of a child's thumbnail. Tabitha pressed her thumb into the coin, hard, and released it, looking for the imprint, but nothing was left. She tried it again, harder even this time, but still nothing. The violence of the movement escalated. What struck her again and again was amazement that she could try so hard and still come up empty.

The man of the dented whirligig was husband number one, or so Rosa said, although in her later years Tabitha doubted that he ever was a husband. He could have been her father, although this wasn't a fact she wanted borne out, so it remained a mystery. He was a big man, but one of those big men with dainty legs, white-skinned, almost hairless. In the summer it was always a surprise to see them poking out from his shorts, like straws holding up a giant barrel. Even his feet were dainty, and he took exquisite pleasure in lining up his shoes, narrow, shined and pointy at the toes. Tabitha thought of him as a spider, with a big, fat body and thin, quickly moving legs. By contrast her mother was slow, slow and round and dense, like a heavy loaf of bread. Her hair was smooth and dark, and her eyes were the colour of ripe green olives – an Italian beauty folded in a thick wrapper of flesh. Next to each other, Tabitha thought Rosa's pale-faced husband looked like a maggot.

Over the years and as she made her way through husbands, Rosa's weight went up and down – down in the early throes of love, as she got thin enough for her hipbones to jut out from satin skirts slit to the thigh while she leaned against a kitchen counter watching the latest man huddle over her spaghetti and homemade sausage – and up again once the affair became routine, while she scrubbed away at the hardened red sauces clinging to the pots, stopping every so often to dry her hands and pop something sweet or salty into her mouth. Tabitha learned early – to love was to be thin and undernourished, ecstasy was the sweet sighing of love whistling across your bones as your skin shivered barely on the surface. It had nothing to do with the heart.

Rosa took Tabitha and left her first husband one spring, and Tabitha remembered jumping in every available puddle while Rosa held her stiffly by the hand, squeezing so tight it hurt, and half dragging her, she was moving so fast. Tabitha remembered the white shoes caked in mud, and the dappled effect of mud splats on her mother's legs. For a while they stayed at a strip motel, living on pizza and doughnuts, until one night, charmed by the bright lights and promise of the Texas-style bar across the street, Rosa left Tabitha in a kind of trance and tottered across the street in her high-heeled shoes to husband number two. Max Geller drove a truck, and adored them both, until one night he plunged it over the interstate and straight into the river. That particular state of ecstasy had lasted about six months.

By now Tabitha's mother had acquired a certain kind of seedy worldliness that some men found red hot – especially professional men, and Tabitha recalled that period in her mother's life as a procession of shrinks, professors, and once even a judge. Rosa got a ton of money from Max, who it turned out was no ordinary truck driver but the son of wealthy, if not aloof parents who thought their son was a lawyer in California. With some of the money Rosa enrolled in courses at the university – art history, restoration drama, anything that looked serious. Like a creature from another planet Rosa got special attention and did almost no work, citing her tragic history every time a paper was turned in late or not at all. She began to fall for her Philosophy professor, at least twenty years her senior, and sat in rapt attention as he spoke about Plato, Aristotle, the Golden Mean. He was Greek and something about his dark moustache, his toffee-coloured skin and his endless fascination with analyzing everything stirred her Mediterranean blood. As she got up awkwardly from the modular desks of the university classrooms her hipbones banged against the Formica and she had to slide out provocatively, thrusting her pelvis forward in the direction of her intended target. Costas began coming home for dinner, spaghetti with feta now, and late night reading-aloud of Kavakis and Elytis. Tabitha fell asleep to the sound of their conversations, their literary foreplay:

> Love
> The network of islands
> And the prow of its foam
> And the gulls of its dreams
> On its highest mast a sailor
> Whistles a song.
> Love
> Its song
> And the horizons of its voyage
> And the sound of its longing
> On its wettest rock the bride

Waits for a ship.
Love
Its ship and the nonchalance of its winds
And the jib sail of its hope
On the lightest of its waves an island
Cradles the arrival.

Tabitha loved to listen to the rumble of their voices as she drifted off to sleep at night. Sometimes he read to her at night too, long, luxurious poems translated from the Greek, which she didn't understand, but which lulled her into sleep. There was a soothing quality to Costas, at least as far as Tabitha was concerned, and so she failed to notice how irritated Rosa was becoming with every probing question. Costas was a relentless academic. What do you think of this line? What do you think Plato really meant by the cave? Is it true? Is it how you live? Is it how you might aspire to live? Is it possible? I want to know what you think. I want to know how you feel. I want to know everything. Long after Costas had left, Rosa told Tabitha that when she thought she might be pregnant, she courted the nightmarish thought of Costas at her bedside during delivery. In between shrieks she imagined she could hear his voice rattling off questions – how does it feel? Where exactly is the pain? How do you feel about me right now? What are your thoughts? She pictured peering at him through one half-shut eye in mid- contraction, stroking his irritating little moustache.

But as a child, Tabitha couldn't fathom the stress all this probing put on her mother. For her, the absence of shouting and violence was like waking up every day in a beautiful open field, no fences, no barbed wire, no underground mines you had to make your way around. For her, Costas was childhood – the absence of worry. And so as Rosa chewed her nails down through centuries of Greek philosophers, Tabitha played hopscotch and skipped rope and forgot for a while the elegant lists which up until then had so ordered and calmed her turbulent world.

Costas already had three degrees, including two post-graduate, when he met Rosa, and he was working on his fourth. He seemed to have been born with an incessant need to study, something which Tabitha could easily relate to, but which Rosa had more difficulty with. Tabitha had not been prepared for Costas to leave, and watched with disbelief as the seeds of his departure took root over dinner.

"You know, it seems to me that it would be very good for all of us if you got yourself a nice little job and I could continue to study and we could all live together like a nice regular family." As Costas said this a few small crumbs of feta cheese flicked off his moustache and landed on Rosa's plate, most of the food on which she hadn't even touched. She glanced down at the crumbs, and then over to Costas, who was tucking in obliviously, unaware of the impact of this last statement. Tabitha felt her heart leap – a nice, regular family!

"Why should I get a nice little job? You're the one with all the degrees." She spat this last line out with such venom that expletives would have been superfluous.

"But I don't want a job. I like to study." Costas had no idea that he was sealing in the walls of his fate, brick by brick. "You should get the job."

By now Rosa was wolfing down her food, each forkful getting bigger as she got more angry. "I like to study too. Why should I support you?" Tabitha sat quietly, twirling her spaghetti round and realizing that it would soon be time to move on again.

"I'm afraid your vision of the future isn't mine, Rosa." He turned to Tabitha, who had one small tear rolling down her cheek. "I'll miss you, little one." She went to get up and leave the table, not wanting to see Costas go. But he was already standing, standing and turning his back to them, heading for the door. She didn't want to say goodbye. She didn't want to say anything. A large block of ice had taken up residence somewhere deep inside Tabitha's heart. She didn't know who she hated more, Costas, or her mother, at that moment. She had come that close to a normal life, and she had watched it disappear again, because her mother was stubborn. Why couldn't she go out and get a job? The list of men in her mother's life was getting dull. Tabitha needed to begin devising more interesting lists of her own.

To cheer her up, Rosa had bought a house, and for this at least Tabitha was grateful. It was small, but at least it was in the middle of other houses, part of a community, with other families and kids and it had the outward appearance of normal. Tabitha was tough, tougher than the other kids, and they were all a little afraid of her. She was fearless and knew about cigarettes and sex and the way to please herself long before any of the others. The exoticism of boyfriends and lovers and strange cars parked overnight in the driveway was the very opposite of what Tabitha wanted from the street, and yet it was the lure that drew the street to her.

Tabitha had carried this "otherness" with her all the way to St Simons, where academia barely flickered an eyelid. Everyone there was "other," especially in the Political Science Department. Taped to her door Tabitha had a quote from Fourier, "It is a rule in Harmony that all manias shall be equal before the law." And while the university was no Utopia, the manias were rampant. Tabitha's relatively minor obsession with lists was mostly something that went on in private, and so went unnoticed. Others were more obvious. Speck was unable to throw anything away, and so his office was so piled with books and papers the fire inspectors had to be called in to make sure it wasn't a hazard. Fire or floor collapse, Tabitha wasn't sure which kind it was.

There were others, of course. Morris Blacking was prone to wearing bandages wrapped around different parts of his body, the imaginary wounds shifting from one limb to another depending on the day of the week. Fred Poolsey was always smiling, no matter what the occasion. Once in a while he forgot to put in his teeth, and then it was really embarrassing. But they were all highly revered specialists in their fields, smart men and women, barrelfuls of knowledge. Still, it was a dark kind of cage that

Tabitha found herself in. There were no real compatriots, no soul-mates, now that the women had roundly dumped her and she couldn't see men except as sexual conquests. It was Fourier who kept her alive, Fourier, who had been a travelling salesman by day and who sweated out his elaborate theories and schemes by night, dreaming of his perfect community of elevated souls.

Tabitha was at MacDonald's Dry Cleaners the next morning before they even opened, at 8:55 a.m. She had seen Brian leave in his car, and followed him. She watched him pull into the spot reserved for him behind the building, not that there were ever that many cars at the dry cleaners in Chisholm at any one time. She watched him as he entered the building, watched like a child at a magic show as the lights came on, a kind of fluorescent aurora borealis spreading from one side of the window to the other. The minute he turned the closed sign round to open she was at the door, her fragrant parcel tucked under her arm.

"Good morning! I guess I'm your first customer!"

Brian turned from behind the counter, his thinning and highly ordinary hair luminous in the light, a wad of dry-cleaning receipts in his hands.

"Tabitha! I've never seen you in here before. Was there something you needed to discuss about your portfolio? We can make another appointment."

Tabitha grinned. "No, no, it's not my finances. You see, I'm here with a bit of a dilemma."

"A dilemma?"

Tabitha had found that people in Chisholm were fond of repeating back to you what you'd just said, as a way to buy time. It didn't bother her when it was Brian who did the repeating.

"Yes. You see normally I wash all my smalls..." and here Tabitha permitted herself a small blush, " ...I wash them by hand, but lately, they don't seem to be coming out as well as they used to. I thought...perhaps..."

She held out a small, peach-coloured bikini panty, pure silk, with tiny ties on the sides and a triangle of see-through lace in the middle.

"Perhaps this could be dry-cleaned."

They both stared at the peachy little aid to cuckoldom held between them, suspended like a sudden intake of breath. No one moved. Finally Tabitha pushed it into Brian's stunned hands, and closed his fingers over the soft fabric.

"Just give it a try, would you?"

"I...uh...well I suppose...I..."

"Thanks. You're a sweetheart."

Tabitha blew him a little kiss and turned back towards the door, a cloud of scent in her wake. Giddy with what she imagined would be the success of her plan, she banged into Nathaniel Speck, who was walking along the side of the road, muttering to himself, and not paying any attention at all.

"Oh Tabitha, I'm so terribly sorry. Are you all right?"

There was that voice again, melodious, dark, low, and intense, a voice to go to battle for. Tabitha always had to remind herself where it was coming from, as she straightened out her clothes and looked up into Nathaniel's bulky face.

"I'm fine, really, I wasn't looking either."

Tabitha realized she'd hardly seen Nathaniel since the night of the letters, except across corridors rushing to lectures, his big heavy feet thudding on the ground like the approach of a distant dinosaur. She had to admit she found the letters intriguing, but she couldn't let on that she knew, that she knew he had a secret life as palpable as her own, a belief in an idea strong enough to turn you slightly unbalanced.

"That night, you know, I never had a chance to thank you, Tabitha. It was enormously kind. I shall never forget it."

"It was what anyone would have done. Especially since I'm going to be your neighbour!"

Nathaniel laughed.

"Hah! It was what no one else would have done." He frowned. "Neighbour?"

Tabitha decided that she could probably listen to Nathaniel talk all day, so seductive and inviting were the deep tones of his voice, and the cadence of his speech, a cadence that was almost catching.

"Yep. I bought the land beside yours. You're going to be living right next to the embodiment of one of the nineteenth century's most inspired visions. Harmony, right here in good old Chisholm."

Out of the blue Nathaniel began to hum a little tune. The tune got wider, and bigger, and Tabitha was impressed by the quality of Nathaniel's singing voice, its lilt and timbre like a soothing balm to a wound. "What is that?"

"French poem. Thirteenth century. I'm setting some to music. A little song cycle for the choir."

"I had no idea you were into music."

"Into music. Tabitha, you must do something about your vocabulary. Into this, into that, like a screw into an unrelenting piece of wood."

Tabitha flinched a little at the analogy, barely steps away from MacDonald's Dry Cleaners.

"Yes, well, I guess I've picked that one up from my students."

"Like head lice."

Neither Tabitha or Nathaniel seemed inclined to move on. The day was spreading before them, the town of Chisholm holding up its end by offering a small pleasant wind and a bright Maritime sun, the sound of their voices jumbling musically in the air, and the slow parade of slow-moving Chisholm vehicles passing by them. Nathaniel returned to Tabitha's earlier idea.

"So, you're still obsessed with that Fourier fellow."

"Fraid so. But I've moved outside France now. I'm doing some research into Brook Farm. One of the more workable phalanxes. Good model for the one I'm going to build next to your property."

Nathaniel nodded and grunted, scratched his cheek. He didn't seem to object to the idea of a communal affair being built on his doorstep.

"That word – phalanx. It's really quite unfortunate, isn't it? Sounds like a military formation, or something to do with a penis."

Tabitha laughed.

"Yeah, you're right. Sounds better in French, I guess. Sounds better when Jean-Pierre says it."

And here Tabitha didn't bother to enlighten Nathaniel on the circumstances during which Jean-Pierre uttered the word under discussion. She paused for a moment of reflection.

"It's from the Greek, you know. And it does refer to a formation of soldiers, among other things."

"I thought so. And aren't phalanges the bones that form the fingers and toes. Same word?"

"Yes, exactly. But it's come to mean any kind of association, people, things, whatever."

Nathaniel nodded, and then felt a vague restlessness.

"I'd better be moving along, Tabitha, I've got to write out the parts for that de Blois thing."

Tabitha realized she'd paused for longer than she thought.

"Okay, Nathaniel. Anytime you want to talk about phalanxes, or phalanges, just give me a call."

Good God. What had she just done? Said? Been thinking? Had she just suggested a date? With Nathaniel Speck? No, no, no, she cleared her mind for some introspection. Just two academic colleagues getting together for some scholarly discussion, that was it. What could be wrong with that?

Nathaniel raised both eyebrows, and then dropped them again into a frown, unsure of how to respond. Unable to formulate a reply, he simply said nothing, turned, and returned to his muttering. Tabitha waved, and then felt silly, because he was turned the other way, and so she brought her hand back awkwardly to her hair, and tried to pat it down, hoping no one was looking.

She walked back to her car, and glancing at Brian's parked car, wondered what had become of her underwear.

It was a good night for research. There were no demons lurking in the clouds, no financial appointments, no other commitments. She was writing up a paper on Fourier's Law of Passionate Attractions. Like Fourier, Tabitha couldn't help but agree that most of the problems between people were caused by faulty social arrangements. Marriage was one of them – doomed from the start by its fundamental inability to respect the multiple passions of people like Tabitha. Under Fourier's system, Tabitha wouldn't have to resort to all of this game playing of seduction, all this subterfuge and lying. Why should people have to live on such Spartan gruel, to use Fourier's own words? Tabitha began writing furiously, passionately, harmoniously, her long, pale face lit up a ghastly blue by the computer screen. The Butterfly Passion. It was one of her favourite parts of Fourier's doctrine – the need for periodic change, felt every two hours as acutely as a thorn in the side. Without it being satisfied – the punishments of indifference and boredom.

Tabitha was sure this was what guided and governed her, had her roaming from man to man, restless, energetic, ultimately disappointed. Rather Fourier and his scholarly categorizations of nature and personality than dealing with her own history, most of which she tried to forget. Passionate attractions were just natural drives, unfettered by duty or reason. She was just following the God-given tendencies of anyone of her ilk. And speaking of ilks, Fourier had neatly summed up most of them. A harmonious blend of the various different types of personality would make for a harmonious blend in Utopia. There were solitones, branded by the dominance of any one passion. Academia was likely stuffed to the brim with solitones, but who could she count on to make up the communal bliss she envisaged?

She needed bitones, possessed of two spiritual passions, mixed bitones, one spiritual passion, two sensual, and so on, and so on.

It was all very organized. Tabitha thought of herself as a model polygone, the most interesting of the profiles, and the most complex – dominated by more than one paltry passion. But where were the rest of the polygones? She secretly hoped Brian might be one – simply a repressed one.

As she listed out the types, she tried to picture anyone, anyone at all in Chisholm who might fit any of them and also be receptive to her Utopian ideals. As soon as she entered a name, she deleted it. She was making her way rapidly through every department in the university, without much success. It was a big idea, she recognized, huge – not just a paper destined for musty retirement in the library, but a living, breathing, working community! The whole idea had her fired up but with nowhere to go. Passions left unfulfilled were dangerous, so Fourier had said. Passions and manias had to be employed, their energy put to good use. The phalanx was the place to start! The phalanx!

Tabitha wore herself out on nights like these, probing through Fourier's writings, translating some of them from the original French, figuring out what went wrong when the ideas were picked up in America. And always at the back of her mind was the idea that she could get Fourier right, as no one else had, make his ideas work, restore him to his rightful historical place by grounding him in the twenty-first century. It was the one idea that kept her going, that sustained her on the long nights in Chisholm when all the other lights down the street had been turned off, when children, parents, and grandparents, solitones, bitones, and hepatones, had turned in for the night and were snoozing and dreaming in their beds, and when the loneliness of her energies, her enthusiasm and her passions, completely misunderstood, was too much to bear.

Tabitha waited a suitable few days before returning to Brian's for her peach panties. She wanted to give him time to linger over them, fondle them, sneaking into the back room and bringing them to his nose in a rapt state of ecstasy. She desperately wanted to believe that he was a creature capable of passion, not the mindless sex she had settled for in the past. She kept herself busy with class preparation and research into Fourier. She was still trying to figure out how to deal with a student who had discovered Fourier's prediction that eventually, members of the phalanx would grow tails. Naturally Tabitha knew about it, had had to wrestle with it herself, but she didn't want it to obscure what Fourier was saying elsewhere. She believed in the law of passionate attractions, believed people were dominated by drives they were born with, and she believed that passions held down by civilized society could easily turn vicious. Besides, he appealed to her innate sense of order. Fourier was the consummate listmaker! Combined order a synonym for harmony!

But then there was this tail business. Fourier was a colourful writer, with a knack for analogy. She would have to take it on this level to make it work, to win back the respect of one of her brighter students. It wasn't often a student would read outside the given readings and required texts, and she wasn't about to lose him. She would explain to him about the apples, about Adam, and Paris, and Newton – and Fourier! How a single apple had cost his dining companion one hundred *sous*, when better apples were sold by the hundred for fourteen! There must be something terribly wrong with the economics of society for this to happen, Fourier reasoned, and so began his analysis. So you see, she would explain, it wasn't really about the apples, that was just a vehicle. And so it wasn't really about the tails either. He didn't really mean they would grow tails, any more than he meant the ocean would turn to lemonade. But even that was defensible. You had to look at his entire cosmological vision for it to make sense. At the source of it was the passionate life of the entire universe. That would be it, tomorrow's lecture. Once the universe enters into a period of perfect harmony, Tabitha scribbled, a great ring will form around the North Pole, known as The Northern Crown. This ring will be in constant contact with the sun, warming the polar ice cap and stabilizing the climate. The nature of the seas will change, losing their salt and producing – a sort of lemonade. Had he predicted global warming, for God's sake?

Of course dealing with the tails and the lemonade was one thing, but she had to sidestep an even wider range of predictions, wherein, in an era of perfect harmony:

–androgynous plants would mate;
–six moons would orbit the earth;
–people would speak in blank verse;
–the world would contain 37 million poets equal to Homer, 37 million mathematicians equal to Newton, and 37 million dramatists equal to Molière, although these were, after all, mere estimates.

Okay, she had to admit it, Fourier did sound a trifle eccentric. But she believed, with a passionate fervour, that at the core of it was the truth, even if all around it was chaos. Tabitha began her notes on The Northern Crown. But the ideas began to flee as soon as they presented themselves, like a family of mice into their respective holes, and Tabitha kept dropping off. Brian's face kept appearing in her mind, where a series was meant to be, his innocent hands appeared where she was hoping for a comfortable list – say, the vices of commerce?

Just then a flashing message appeared on her screen, telling her she had new mail.

"the thing about utopia? it's always somewhere else, tabitha, and when you get there, it's already moved on. don't waste your time on this. it's no more than a theory. rosa."

How like her mother to be hip already to the e-mail practice of avoiding caps. Tabitha pressed reply real quick, but the message disappeared. Another opportunity lost. Sometimes Tabitha wondered if Rosa didn't hang on to Tabitha's guilt like a perpetually wet rag, endlessly wringing it out for what it was worth.

Tabitha decided to wander down to the dry cleaners. It was near closing time, and she would likely be the only customer.

The nights were beginning to close in now, and the sky and the clouds took on the hues of storm-tossed sea blues and inky purples, the beauty and the menace of the maritime winter to come. Tabitha layered on an extra sweater and paused for a moment to fix her hair. She'd had it cut in a china bob, and died it black for a change, which gave her a dramatic, city look. She was pleased with the effect of her dark hair set against the yellow sweater. She walked down the street to MacDonald's Dry Cleaners, striding like a champion, and filled with a kind of sweet curiosity about how she would be greeted, about what might have now changed between her and the object of her academic pursuit.

By the time she got there, it was almost dark, but the warm and welcoming lights of the dry cleaners were still on. From across the road she could see Brian at the till, counting out his take for the day and making notations on a pad of paper. She stood and watched him, as the pedestrian sign changed several times from stop to go and back again, and hesitated. Who knew which way Brian would go if left to the freedom of his own drives and desires in Harmony? Who even knew what they were? Maybe that was what really intrigued her. It had been easy to root out the weaknesses in most of the men she had managed to bed down, like a pig sniffing out truffles in the dank woods. But Brian, now there was another story. Brian was so straight, so earnest, so endearing. When he spoke about financial planning, he spoke about financial planning. When he asked Tabitha how things were going, that's all he meant.

She crossed the street and opened the door, as a little bell rang. Brian looked up, and then it appeared to Tabitha that his face turned slightly pink, but she could have been mistaken. She smiled a broad smile, and approached the counter. Melamine was all that separated them.

"Tabitha! You're in late."

Brian cleared his throat several times and straightened the receipts into a perfect square. Tabitha had to admit she still got a tiny thrill hearing him say her name.

"I was working at my desk and I just had to get out for some air, Brian, you know how it is. God, it is hot in here though, isn't it."

Tabitha pulled off her sweater and waved the edge of her blouse towards him, releasing some "Poeme" fragrance into the air, where it mixed with the sulfuric smell of the dry-cleaning fluids and solutions and choked quickly to death.

"I'm afraid there was a problem with your last, uh, order. I guess the machines aren't really set up for anything that small. I should have known, really."

Brian went under the counter and pulled out something that resembled a shredded bit of Kleenex. Awkwardly, he held it out to her, and as she put out her hand, he dropped it in. They both stared at it, and then Tabitha raised her face just as Brian raised his. Their faces almost touched, and they stared right into each other's eyes. It was hard to say who moved first or even what prompted it – but suddenly Tabitha's lips were pressed into Brian's. It was a kiss that Tabitha imagined to be the culmination of so many passions long held back that it quite took her breath away and when she finally had to pull back, if only for air, she had completely forgotten where she was. Main Street. Chisholm. Glass storefront.

Brian seemed to realize it at the very same moment, and he motioned her round to the side of the counter where he unhitched the latch and she slid through into the hidden world behind the counter. Brian went to the door, locked it, and turned the sign round from open to closed. The little bell rang again as he did it, and for a moment he hesitated too, as Tabitha had done from across the street. He turned off all but the small desk light on the counter and ran to her. Spread out before him on the dark green marbled tiles she looked like a goddess, her dark nipples as luscious as chocolate and her skin as perfect as a pressed white shirt. He dropped down on her like a man released from prison, and was almost spent before he even got inside her. They lay like that until the cold floor began to press into Tabitha's back, and Brian's weight threatened to suffocate her. She pushed him off roughly, and he woke up with a start. He straightened up and his head disappeared into the rainfall of plastic dry-cleaning bags that hung down from the rack. He began brushing them aside but they clung like sticky cobwebs. They didn't really know what to say to each other. Brian spoke first.

"Next time, let's do it in a bed."

The silence between them was vast and oppressive. Tabitha put her clothes back on furtively while Brian closed up the shop. Brian didn't drive her home; they decided it was probably best to leave separately. Once outside, she watched his back as he walked towards his car, thinking how often she had faced the backs of men, turning away. As Tabitha walked slowly back up the hill towards home, she puzzled over her reaction to everything that had happened in the past few hours.

She couldn't say she felt disappointed, any more than she felt elation, or satisfaction, or anger, or revenge, or any emotion at all. There had been this rush of sex, but all around it was a vast empty space. So what else was new? She had managed to seduce him, but what did it prove? Only that he was like every other man she had met, and not the unique candidate for harmonious association she had stupidly willed him to be. In her heart, she didn't really know if she had wanted him to be seduced, or not. She had given it her all, that was sure, but now that it had happened, there was a confusing anticlimax.

The sky began a low rumble, and she pulled her sweater in tighter, refused to look up at the sky in case Rosa might appear, a huge mouth spread out like a constellation and the words popping out like shooting stars "I told you so!"

She could feel the spears of winter hurtling through the air, and she fought hard not to think of some of the Maritime storms she had encountered over the years in Chisholm – snow heaped up right past the windows of her little house, the blinding frenzy of blowing snowflakes making her feel as if she were inside one of those glass balls you turn upside down and shake until you can no longer see the tiny plastic figures trapped inside. She remembered the walls of snow so high on either side of her driveway she could scarcely heave the shovel with enough gusto to get the new snow over the top. And one morning, unable to shovel for a moment longer and sick of having most of the snow topple off again, she simply threw the shovel on the ground, and walked to the university. When she reached the grounds she headed straight for the bathroom and found that most of her mascara had run down her face and on to her cheeks. Alice Cooper, she thought, I've turned into a ghoul, as she tried to scrub it off with warm water and scratchy paper towels.

Once she reached the top of the hill she turned left on to her street, and walked past Laura and Brian's house. She looked up at the windows and saw some movement, the boys passing back and forth in their pyjamas probably, brushing their teeth, getting ready for bed. Brian's car was already in the driveway, and she wondered what he had said to explain why he was so late coming back from work. He had driven by her as she walked up the hill, but hadn't honked or waved. Tabitha considered how easily and how ordinarily Brian's life had simply returned to itself, the practised patterns of bedtime, Daddy at each bedside saying goodnight and kissing them on their foreheads, Laura standing at the doorway, arms folded, knowing what comes next, and the same after that, and after that.

Tabitha's house loomed before her a little further down the street, no lights on, no welcoming arms there, only a cold late supper of tinned salmon and a little salad. And her wide empty bed, the thought of which had never before felt so empty, so deserted, and so dismal. As she turned the key in the lock, she thought she heard some shouting from down the street, but she decided it was probably from the corner variety store on the far side of the field across from her house, the hangout for local teenagers who had nowhere else to go. She opened the door, and stepped into the gloom.

Days went by before she heard from him. She consumed herself with work, trying to figure out what had happened, or even what she had expected. She was forced to admit that theorizing about Brian's seduction had been a lot more satisfying than carrying it through. Then one day Tabitha picked up the phone in her office unawares.

"Hello. Professor Black speaking."

"Tabitha, it's Brian. What are you doing?"

At that particular moment, Tabitha was lying back in her chair, her legs up and her slender feet resting on a pile of mid-term essays in the middle of her desk. It was a pretty safe bet that at least three quarters of them would be about the same thing, "Was the Garden of Eden a Real Utopia?" even though Tabitha had given them four other more interesting, although difficult choices. Marking papers was one of the necessary chores she had to undertake as a professor, but it was also one of the more hateful. For no matter how interesting the topics she came up with, somehow the majority of papers always ended up being spectacularly uninteresting in their treatment of the subject – boiling everything down to the prim minimum, with sentences constructed as if from a child's first reader. Now and again there were exceptions, but they were few and far between. She'd tried several approaches to dealing with essays, but none of them was successful. She tried marking them in huge batches, slogging away day and night until they were done, but that left her in a fitful state of exhaustion. Then she'd tried marking no more than five a day, for a period of several weeks, but then the process seemed to drag on forever. There seemed to be no happy medium.

"I'm uh, I'm actually marking papers. Mid-terms."

She sat back up in her chair and took her feet off the pile, grabbing the first few on top as if to try to make true what she had just said.

"The house is empty. Laura's gone off to her sister's out in Pomquet, and the kids are all at school. Can you come over?"

"I've got quite a few to mark here."

Being Brian's mistress wasn't what she had in mind. And rather than prove anything useful about Fourier's theories, all Brian had succeeded in doing was muddling her brain.

"I really want to see you. Couldn't you just finish those later?"

"I could probably finish these later. But look, Brian..."

But Brian had already clicked off.

Tabitha decided to park her car at her house and walk down to Brian's. She stopped off first for a bottle of wine and noticed Laura in the coffee shop at the far end of Main Street, where the Liquor Store and Tim Hortons provided dual forms of solace. She almost jumped back seeing Laura, who was supposed to be in Pomquet. Laura looked the way she always did, fresh and young somehow, wearing pale blue and a wide band that pulled her blond hair back from her achingly earnest face. She was drumming her hands on the side of her coffee cup, and making notes on a placemat. Tabitha wondered what she could possibly be doing. She hadn't seen her, being too absorbed in whatever she was writing, so she decided to leave well enough alone and move on. She arrived at the doorway of Number 1212 Pleasant Valley Drive with an unassuming Merlot tucked under her arm, and what she planned as a message from Fourier.

When Brian opened the door, she noticed he was wearing a pale blue shirt too, probably picked out by Laura, and she felt dimly uncomfortable, suddenly seeing Laura's face there before her. But the moment of self-examination soon passed and she stepped inside, as Brian closed the door behind her.

"We need to talk. I've brought a nice little wine here, a California..."

But Brian wasn't interested in pleasantries or in wine. He began fumbling with her buttons while at the same time trying to guide her upstairs to the bedroom. Tabitha followed along, so familiar with the rites of seduction she barely knew what she was doing, until they reached the top of the stairs. By now she was partially undressed and totally uninterested in lovemaking. As Brian groped for the rest of her clothes she looked over at Laura and Brian's bed. It was as fresh, trim and tidy as Laura herself; she could see that it had been made, at least partly. The blanket and the top sheet were in a heap on the floor, but the fitted sheet contained barely a ripple, and the corners were tucked in perfect symmetry. The whole, wide, smooth and available expanse of it seemed to clear Tabitha's mind of all troubles, all doubts, all common sense, and together they tumbled on to it, Brian by now making his way through his own buttons and paraphernalia. Once again there wasn't much in the way of foreplay and Brian was on top of her in seconds. She tried rolling him over, so she could get on top, but he was surprisingly heavy and she couldn't shift him, and then she tried twisting beneath him to get in a better position, but it was too late, it was over. He lay there again, like a slain animal, as she struggled to breathe. Finally he inched sideways and she seized her chance to push him off. She began feeling cold, and reached over the end of the bed for the blanket. In doing so, she pulled the top end of the sheet off with her feet, and the rest of it rippled together accordion style. She tried to stretch it back, but it kept popping off, so she gave up and curled away from him under the blanket. Brian had dropped immediately off to sleep, and was loudly snoring beside her. Ahead of her on the large chest of drawers was a crowd of photographs, an accusatory mob of MacDonald relations – children in white confirmation dresses, Brian and Laura in their wedding photo, framed by the yawning vagina of a tree, and Brian and Laura's graduation pictures, complete with ridiculous looking hats. What the hell are you doing, they seemed to be saying in chorus. Tabitha couldn't look the photographs in the eye.

Laundry had been piled and sorted into whites and colours by the doorway, and there were some toys innocently placed behind the laundry basket, reminding her there were children living in this house. Tabitha didn't know what to think about children, having grown up so early and been an adult for so long. And she reminded herself that Fourier hadn't wanted to eliminate the passion of the family, he just wanted to recreate it in a less repressive form.

Tabitha dropped her hand down by the edge of the bed where it plopped into a half finished glass of what looked and smelled like and was sticky enough to be Cherry Kool-Aid. She recoiled and shook the drops at Brian, who stirred only slightly, and then she peered down on a book left face down and open, the edges of the cover turned up like the roof of a Chinese pagoda: *Mutual Funds: Economic Survival or Financial Disaster*.

Whether by design or by desperation, Tabitha could feel the slow-moving tide of a list coming on, and there wasn't a thing she could do about it. The whole experience was like the coming of a migraine – her forehead got cool and clammy, the light from the window turned cruel and piercing, and she felt as if the skin on her skull was shifting and tightening, pressing down on her nerves. She tried to set aside the formation of her own, inevitable list by focusing on Fourier's hierarchy of cuckolds. But her head was muddled. In Fourier's descriptions, was it the man who was the cuckold to his wife's adulterous liaisons, or the other way round. What was the female equivalent? A cuckette? She tried to think clearly, but the list began to unscroll in her head and she was powerless to stop it. It went something like this:

- owing to her ridiculous habits of seduction, by now Brian has come to think of her as a slut;
- owing to his ridiculous habits of seduction, Brian now fancies himself a ladies' man and will become hopelessly conceited and impossible to be with, no candidate for Harmony;
- Laura, having consulted with a guru, has come to her senses, recognized her true value in life, and decided to leave Brian and set up shop on her own, with the kids, and Brian will become heartsick and good for nothing but

bitter self-reproach (or worse, self-pity), still no good for Harmony;

– Laura, having consulted with a guru, has discovered the affair and is heading there now with a large butcher knife.

The sound of a door slamming downstairs broke the momentum of Tabitha's list, and she and Brian sat up stock straight in bed at the same time, like two vampires wakened from their coffins by the smell of blood. Brian had a look of inflamed terror on his face, and Tabitha looked around for a cupboard or somewhere to hide. A booming voice shot up the stairs.

"Mrs. MacDonald? I'm here about the washer. You called me last week."

Brian leaped to his feet and threw on his pants, dashed towards the door. Standing at the bottom of the staircase was a man in blue overalls, and a cap, a huge man who looked vaguely ridiculous wearing overalls, a giant dressed like a child. He looked up as Brian fought for breath and the right thing to say.

"Worked late at the dry cleaners last night. Two of the machines are down. Needed a bit of a rest." The sentences came out staccato, unmistakable evidence of a lie in progress.

"Right enough. Is the washer down in the basement?"

"Yes, the light's at the top of the stairs. I'll be right there and explain the trouble we've had."

The man had already turned and was walking away towards the stairs. He muttered as he left.

"No problem sir. Take your time."

It was the sir that did Brian in. He stepped back inside the bedroom where Tabitha was already dressed and brushing her hair with Laura's brush. A few dark hairs caught up with Laura's blond ones. Tabitha didn't look over as she spoke.

"I didn't know you left your front door open."

Brian picked up the brush as soon as Tabitha set it down, and began pulling the hairs out of it, tugging frantically until they broke free. She was surprised at the zeal with which Brian was attempting to excise her from his life. He dumped the hair into the wastebasket beside the chest of drawers. Neither of them could look each other in the face.

"Everyone does in Chisholm. Nobody locks their door like they do in the city."

"I lock mine."

There was a long and perilous silence, into which was dumped, without ceremony, the entire fantasized contents of Tabitha's communal life with Brian. They both stared into the wastebasket, as if they expected a genie to pop out and grant them three wishes. What Brian wanted was to just return to his old life, to keep things simple. It had been nothing more than a temporary fit, a blip.

"Look, I just can't do this, Tabitha, I'm sorry."

There was a huge bang from the basement, and then the sound of water sloshing animatedly through pipes. Brian sat down on the edge of the bed. He decided to appeal to Tabitha's compassion.

"My family – they are just too dear to me."

"That's not what you were thinking a few moments ago," Tabitha found herself saying aloud.

"Well, I like you, of course I do. And listen, the sex was really great."

Those last familiar words shot through Tabitha like a bolt of lightning. She began to feel faint. She had created this whole ridiculous and humiliating scenario entirely on her own, and now she was going to have to suffer through it. Why had she deluded herself again? Why hadn't she recognized what an idiot she had been? Why had she thrown herself at yet another man who didn't want her?

"I think I have to get out of here. I have to get some air."

Brian sprung to his feet.

"Just let me check the landing."

Brian peered down the stairs and turned back to her.

"Coast is clear."

It was an inappropriately jaunty expression for the moment. Tabitha came and stood beside him. She wasn't going to get a goodbye hug, or even a look of wistful longing for what might have been.

"What are you going to do, Tabitha? You know, at your age, the chances of finding someone to hook up with are about the same as getting struck by lightning twice in the same year."

Brian said this with all the matter-of-fact disinterest with which he quoted stock figures or investment strategies. Tabitha doubted that he even meant to be unkind. But suddenly it became even clearer that Brian was not at all the sort of man she wanted to embark on her life's dream with.

"Marriage is a plague on both sexes." She patted down her hair, flicked a dark strand from her sweater, called on her soulmate for a spot of dignity in a moment of extreme humiliation. "Fourier – Philosophy, Morality, and Sex in Civilization. Chapter Two, Page 324."

Then Tabitha fled down the stairs and out the door, leaving behind her the broken washer, the piles of sorted and unsorted laundry, and the complicated weave of a marriage, a fabric she had thankfully, and just in the nick of time, become unravelled from.

Keeping the Past in its Rightful Place

"*There is enormous power in the present – concentration on the task at hand, refusal to be distracted by previous follies, the absence of illusions. Yet sometimes the past comes creeping in, unexpected, unannounced, and you must stuff it back in the baggage hold where it belongs, and move ahead. The past can creep up on you in many forms – even the seemingly innocent wagging of a dog's tail can send you into a torment of once was, once could have been. Don't go there! Live in the glorious present.*"

From *Everyman's Guide to the Modern Universe and Household Management*, Nathaniel P. Speck, Professor of Medieval History, St Simons University, Chisholm, Nova Scotia

Seven

For the time being, Nathaniel had abandoned his ideas of marriage, or at least the idea of ordering a bride from a catalogue. The whole sordid mess of the lobster boil had left him shattered, and spent. So much had been invested in those letters, those precious wonderful letters, which he had to admit, to some extent, had been more satisfying than a relationship. Rashida at a remove was the perfect woman. Nathaniel at a remove was the perfect man. What a splendid theoretical union!

Nathaniel wandered about in his house, pausing for a moment here and there to collect his thoughts. Here was where it was all to have taken place: the anticipated look of wonder on Rashida's face as she inspected one room after another; the peaceful order of Nathaniel's things and the delicacy with which he had left spaces here and there for her; an empty drawer, a wide open shelf; here was the kitchen, where she would introduce Nathaniel to the specialties of her country, and the smells of cardamom pods popping and coriander seeds sizzling would conjure up her home, and for a while she would be sad, until Nathaniel took her into the protection of his arms, where she would feel immediately safe, loved, content.

Nathaniel paused at his collection of books on medieval women. For Nathaniel, the position of women was a pretty good indicator of the extent of civilization. In Nathaniel's ideal world, his twenty-first century middle ages, women would be worshipped. As he had intended to worship his intended. Rashida would have wept great tears of joy and happiness had she known what was in store for her. Had she only given him the chance!

But what a great, blundering idiot he had been. What kind of lover storms the bastion of his wife's first delicate affections smeared with lobster meat and wearing protective goggles? Not to mention brandishing a collection of instruments that would be more appropriate in a torture chamber than a dining room.

Still, first appearances could be deceiving. She could have given me the chance, Nathaniel reasoned, she didn't have to leave immediately on the next flight out. He had checked in with the airlines when she hadn't shown up at his house the next day. He had still believed, waking up under the afghan Tabitha had placed over him like a protective shield, that she might reconsider, at least talk to him. But their entire history was written in letters, and beyond that there was only the silence of what might have been, a heavy, shifting weight that Nathaniel now carried with him like an invisible hunchback.

Lurching towards his study he thought he saw a shadow pass by his front window. Perhaps it was a trick of the lights, a car passing by, a moose or a deer nosing out from beyond the trees. But as Nathaniel rummaged about in his study for a recent book published in German about Hildegard of Bingen, which he was planning to translate in his womanless spare time, he saw it again: a shape blocking the narrow side window, and then gone again, the light driven back in like an arrow. He picked up a rather thick book, something about women and education in the middle ages, and prepared to fight off an intruder, but as he held it up, a thick wad of notes slipped out of the bottom, and he bent over to pick them up and see what they were, temporarily oblivious to what might be someone about to break into his house. His notes on the nunneries – his theory they were medieval powerhouses for women! (Not so, thought Rosa from above, having recently had a very long and revealing conversation with Julian of Norwich). Thank God, thank God! Nathaniel's heart raced. He had been trying to find these notes for months and as he found himself absorbed in re-reading the scribbles and notations begun in a tireless heat one evening last spring, the book references and the factual coincidences all tying together in one tantalizing intellectual parcel extremely suitable for getting a sizeable research grant, he heard a knock. At least he thought it was a knock, so faint and tentative it could have been a heavy blossom brushing against the door. But there was no mistake. Nathaniel looked up again. There it was.

Dropping a few of his notes he headed for the door, and wrenched it open. The shift in the weather had made it stick, but he knew that in a few short weeks it would resolve itself as the first snow began to fall. Through the intricate mesh of Nathaniel Speck's screen door stood someone he never expected to see again, and the last of the nunnery notes that were clutched in his hands withered like fall leaves to the floor. Neither of them moved. A small, chilly wind blew through the screen.

It was Fiona. Released from her cloud-veil of steam and twenty years older, but Fiona all the same. Nathaniel hung back in shock until she finally spoke.

"Cousin, I've given you a turn. I'm sorry. I walked around your place a few times before I had the nerve to knock, but you seemed so preoccupied, I didn't want to give you heart failure!" She laughed, and then thought better of it, because Nathaniel was still standing on the other side of the screen, immobile as a rock.

"Are you planning to leave me out here?"

Nathaniel finally recovered and opened the screen door, stepping aside to let Fiona in. He was just about to close the door behind her when a small, dishevelled black and white dog crept in quickly after her, then cringed and stood shaking behind a chair, trying to hide.

"That's Bill."

What the hell were Fiona and "Bill" doing at his house? All Nathaniel wanted to do just then was go back to his notes, sit down at the computer and look up some of those references again, engage nose to nose with the writings of Julian of Norwich, St Agnes of Bohemia, Hildegard of Bingen. Research was, after all, the great saviour of those totally unsuited for normal life. Hermetic tendencies were praised as studious erudition, rudeness passed for brilliance and eclecticism, you could forget to brush your teeth for weeks on end and fellow scholars would nod their heads as if to say they understood what it was to be in the totally absorbing realm of intellectual discovery, to have day to day routines fly out the window.

But here was Fiona, and from the look of her overstuffed tapestry bag, here was Fiona to stay for a while.

"Where's Dick?" Nathaniel peered around the corner, looking from right to left, half expecting to see Fiona's husband trudging up the hill, and surprised that the first words to have been uttered from his lips after seeing Fiona were about that asshole Dick.

"Dick's history." Fiona snapped, and shut the door behind her.

Fiona hadn't aged all that gracefully, Nathaniel thought later, as they sat together at his kitchen table sharing a pot of Earl Grey. Her now-greying hair had been cut short, like a man's, in a jagged razor cut that meant you could see all the fine hairs at the side of her cheek, and the botched ear piercing which had left a crescent-shaped series of red scars on both ears. Dick's idea, in some perverse desire to return to their youth – they'd both had it done, but Dick's took and Fiona's hadn't, even though she doused the holes every night with peroxide until they burned. Fiona had lost and gained weight so many times the skin didn't know what to do with itself and so it just sort of hung there, in lethargic folds, especially around her neck. Fiona was currently thin, and her clothes looked misshapen, a size or two too large. Nathaniel listened to her, and tried to imagine her as she had been, tried to see behind her pale green eyes what he had once found so intoxicatingly attractive about her.

"Trivets. That's how it started."

Nathaniel settled back for one of those late-night monologues that called for cigarettes and an open bottle of Southern Comfort on the table. Except that he didn't smoke and all he had to drink was Twinings.

"Trivets." He repeated.

"Stuffed with seashells."

"Seashells." Nathaniel was beginning to bore himself, so he sat up straighter in his chair and poured more tea. Fiona's remained untouched.

"That's how he made his money, Lord Almighty, I'm telling you the absolute truth. And did they sell. People would pawn off their grandmothers for one of these things. Taste of the sea. Touch of the Maritimes and all that shit. And there's Dick, he's from fucking Ontario for fuck's sake. Grand Bend for the love of Jesus."

Nathaniel nodded, and Fiona went on.

"So like, now they're selling these things in galleries! Galleries! And Dick thinks he's an artist. And he wants his fucking ears pierced. And a tattoo on my fucking navel."

Fiona gulped down a mouthful of tea and wiped her mouth with the back of her hand.

"That's when the young girls started coming around. Kids, for God's sake. Could he teach them about art, could he show them where to find shells on the beach, could he explain the mysteries of the universe and about fucking. Fucking!"

Fiona's voice was getting louder and louder, and Nathaniel tried to calm her down with some oatmeal cookies, something to do with her hands.

"Did he ever...you know...these girls..."

Despite Fiona's fluency with the word, Nathaniel couldn't bring himself to use it. But he was sufficiently grounded in reality to know that if he said fornication he'd spoil the mood.

"That was the last fucking straw. I found them down on the beach, two of them, all over Dick, and him, laid back there, his fucking earrings sparkling in the sun, big fucking smile all over his face. And he saw me, then, you know, after a couple of minutes, he opened his eyes and he saw me, and you know what he said?"

"I truly can't imagine." Nathaniel replied dryly, wishing he smoked so he'd have something else to think about besides Dick stretched out on the ground with some young vixens crawling all over his body.

"It's all about art. That's what he said. Can you believe it?"

But Nathaniel was still having trouble believing any of this was possible. He was having trouble picturing Dick, short, slightly balding, pale, soft sickly looking Dick, turning into this love God. Piercing his ears. Hanging about galleries. Of course he'd never actually met Dick, only seen pictures which were sent to him by various relatives – the wedding (he'd been invited, but had no intention of going), the two of them pictured outside their new three-bedroom split, Dick with one pale sickly hand on their new Chevy Impala, the other around Fiona's waist.

Nathaniel tried to remember what it was that had so dazzled him about Fiona. Of course she was older, she had had sex! He supposed that she was the stuff of which, if you were fifteen and of Nathaniel's bookish and unusual disposition, dreams were made. And, he was forced to admit, that growing up in such a masculine household, the very fact that she was female made almost everything she did irresistible. He saw her pots and lotions lined up on the dresser in the spare room, turned the lids and breathed in their flowery smells and their softness, and imagined his mother; picked up Fiona's hairbrush, with its soft silken strands wound around the handle, and imagined his mother's hair brushing against his cheek; watched everything Fiona did as if it represented all things womanly, female, maternal.

But if she had been the dream, then who was she now sitting before him, snorting with frustration and denouncing trivets as the root of all the world's evils.

"Anyway, Nathaniel, I know we haven't seen each other for these last thirty years, and I know I've got no call to ask anything of you, but I wondered, just until I get things sorted out, if I could stay here with you. Just until I get my own place. It just seems so fucking peaceful here."

Nathaniel was looking down at Bill, who now looked as if he owned the place, backed up against the wall and blissfully licking his private parts, one hind leg shooting straight up in the air. He looked over at Fiona's tapestry bag, which was resting near the door beside a handful of his notes, and he thought for a moment of Mary Poppins flying through the air with her bag and umbrella to answer the ad for a nanny with a cheerful disposition. He looked over at Fiona, her tear-stained face now red and swollen. Marriage was a plague on both sexes, he recalled Tabitha saying, quoting from Fourier. He reached across the table and took Fiona's hands.

"Stay here as long as you need, my dear. You can have the spare room at the back. The only thing I ask, is that when I'm working in my study, you leave me be."

"Oh thank you, of course, I won't be any bother, I promise, I won't cause you any trouble."

She leaned over and kissed Nathaniel's hands, which he immediately withdrew, and then felt bad about. Already he was beginning to second-guess himself, and that was always the first sign of trouble. But he had no idea of the trouble which lay ahead. As Fiona would have said, no fucking idea.

Ways to Act When Loved Ones Go Astray
      "*If there were neatly formed paths for us to follow, signposted and clearly laid out, we would never go astray. But, at least until you bought this book, dear reader, no such pathways were marked, making the act of veering off almost a way of life. And so, faced with the reality that a loved one has committed some highly human folly, I would caution you against any impetuous acts borne of self-indulgent moral superiority. There but for the luck of the draw, if you'll forgive me the use of the vernacular, go you.*"

From *Everyman's Guide to the Modern Universe and Household Management*, Nathaniel P. Speck, Professor of Medieval History, St Simons University, Chisholm, Nova Scotia

Eight

Laura was still figuring out ways to establish Twisted as some sort of mail-order franchise kit as she pulled into the driveway of her house. Brian was working down at the dry cleaners and the boys were still away, which meant that she would have the entire house to herself, and all of its breathable, calming familiarity to help her nerves, now suddenly on edge due to the enormity of what she had in mind for the business. She pushed the door open and saw the note on the front hall washstand, next to the invoice for the washing machine repairs.

Hi honey,
The washing machine is fixed! Forgot my briefcase this morning and had to come back for it. The guy had it done in less than an hour. Hope you had fun at your sister's.
Love you,
B

Laura read through the note a couple of times and thought about how fortunate she really was to have a husband like Brian. Owing to the business she had had an uncomfortable awakening into the reality of most of the marriages in Chisholm. And even though Brian was a narcissistic bore, at least he was faithful, and he did seem to grasp the sheer domestic joy of having a major household appliance fixed. And then there was the homey familiarity of that "B"– and all the years that went with it, stretching back to that moment she had said "I do," smiling up at him in a kind of trance. Despite the arms of the empty house that reached for her, Laura decided to head for the dry cleaners and pay him a surprise visit. But first, a quick shower and maybe even a spritz of that perfume her mother had given her on her last birthday, a sly little innuendo contained therein – after a few years, dear, men started to stray, you had to remind them of the woman they married.

Laura mounted the stairs two at a time and then stopped with a start as she reached the top and peered into their bedroom. As if a large, dark, and threatening cloud had decided to stop and hover, right outside Brian and Laura's bedroom window, the gravity of the scene blocked out all light and cast the whole room in various shades of grey. Laura was temporarily mummified. The bed she had left that morning was half made, as flat and smooth as calm, untroubled water. A serious flush came over her cheeks as she assessed the truth of what was laid out before her. The bed she now surveyed was in complete turmoil on one side, the corners pulled up and the shameless stitched tapestry of the mattress exposed underneath. One corner of the sheet had been twisted and lurched together like a cotton tornado, and everywhere between there were the folds and wrinkles, the humps, lumps and agitation, of, she was forced to admit it, another woman.

Laura dropped to her knees. She could hardly breathe. She could hardly believe it! Brian had been here, in their bed, with another woman. Everything she had been thinking just before went up in a puff of smoke. For some reason, inexplicable except to a woman who has just found out her husband is having an affair, Laura didn't stand up, but shuffled awkwardly, still on her knees, over to the bed. She couldn't help herself from pulling the sheet corner down and straightening it out, trying to restore the bed's former dignity. God, all those marriages she had chuckled over, and here she was – one of them! She knew she should have made some notes, jotted down the particular shape and pattern of the wrinkles, the height of the lumps, the exact warp and woof of the commotion. But there was no need. From her position on her knees she could see straight into the waste basket, and there it was. Curled up like something unborn was the fibrous mass of hair Brian had pulled from Laura's brush, and those sinuous black strands told Laura exactly who had been in the bed with B. There was only one woman in Chisholm who had such unnaturally black hair.

She felt a faint queasiness in the pit of her stomach. It was one thing to snoop around other people's bedrooms in the stillness of late morning, an air of whispered confidences wrapped around her like a blanket, sharing coffee and secrets and making notes. In fact, that was as good as studying the frogs had been, out in the cool air by herself, layered in fleece and sweaters, nothing but the sounds of the forest around her. No matter that the quiet exchanges she had with her clients could set off a chain reaction of screaming matches, terrible fights, and even divorces. At that singular moment, there was only the pure and absolute evidence of what had been, and was irrefutable.

Same with the frogs. Sure, the remote listening devices and humming attachments she wired to the frogs threw off all systems of communication between them and scrambled their entire hibernation and breeding patterns. But at the time, there was simply the pure, unadulterated joy of research.

For some reason Laura began thinking about the Spring Peeper, as the warm weather approaches and the gradual thaw begins, deep, deep, deep in the core organs. Laura had moved down into the mud at the bottom of a still pond a long time ago, and could probably have survived there forever, in that state of almost-death that most people accept as life and all its bounty. But what if the frog isn't quite ready to leave that place of perfect stillness, she thought. Maybe all that noisy business of heartbeats and breathing just isn't that appealing, compared to the safe and silent world of the deep freeze, the world she had inhabited for so long.

Except that now everything had changed. From that place of perfect silence plots began to hatch and emerge. She had already decided it was time to bring the whole Twisted system to the world. But now she had other plans as well.

It seemed as if Brian had been there, in her life, forever, and suddenly the quality of that foreverness had taken on a whole new twist. Like being strangled with your own scarf. She'd put up with him for so long, making compromises, putting on a brave face. All that wifely stuff she had done. But now, that forever was forever tainted – had there been others? And how could he cheat with that vile academic – that stick-thin little snob. Had it all been a lie? A mistake? Had Brian been looking at her all this time and deciding she wasn't enough? When she herself could hardly stand him? The thought was simply too horrible. To be confronted with the lie of her life this way was beyond reason. She picked herself up and made a beeline for Home Hardware.

Cruising the aisles of the hardware store Laura decided how jaunty all the rows of inflammables looked, lined up on the shelf, in their bright blue and red containers, and she popped them in her cart like children's cereals, Fruit Loops, Cheerios, paint thinner. She had those fabulous long wooden matches at home, the ones Brian's mother had given her to use in the fireplace at Christmas. They were still there, unused, wrapped in their red and green plaid container tube, tied up with a red ribbon. And she had plenty of rags, washed even, the children's old underwear and socks, Brian's white tee-shirts gone grey over the years. She smiled to herself when she thought of those tee-shirts going up in flames, the cotton curling and stretching into a fiendish black grin, the threads splitting and disappearing. She had to admit she liked the idea of consuming flames – their lustiness, their fluidity, and, the thought inescapable, their femaleness.

But where to put the rags, how much stuff to soak them in, how many to use – these were the tough questions. How long would it take? Would there be anything left? Would there be a spectacular blaze or just a lot of smoke? Laura pondered these questions outside Home Hardware, where she paused by her shopping cart for a long-ago forsaken habit, a smoke. Her hands trembled as she removed the first Cameo from its white and green box, the long, cool white perfection of it drawing her back to the first time she smoked one, in high school, behind the temporaries, on a Sunday with her best friend Delia.

Back then she had dreamed of her life with Brian, how they would sell off the dry- cleaning business and move away, to Halifax perhaps, or even Toronto. It was a given that Brian would inherit the business, and it was a given that they would marry. She felt as if she had known him her entire life, and she almost had, but what had made him so appealing back then was the possibility that he could take her away from the life she had always known, the town she had always known. It was so romantic. But back then, taking a long and seductive draw on the cigarette, dreaming of sex and blowing perfect smoke rings into the afternoon, her whole perfect unexplored female self pressed into tight-fitting jeans and a red tee-shirt, Laura hadn't imagined the children, the children who would arrive with alarming speed barely into the first years of marriage. And how suddenly, leaving hadn't seemed like such a good idea, and there were always the children to think about, the children who needed new shoes, new hockey equipment, braces. And so they retreated into their respective roles of husband and wife, barely connected and always together.

She drew out the match, a small, wooden match, from a box with a bright red bird on it, Redbird Matches. She struck it, and she was so absorbed in watching the dance of the orange and yellow flame, almost cross-eyed, she didn't notice Susan, Twisted's very first client, coming up beside her.

"Good God, I never even knew you smoked."

Laura dropped the match with a start and it fizzed into a semi-frozen puddle.

"Susan. You scared me."

"And you me. I always thought you were perfect."

Susan grinned, but Laura ignored her. She was busily trying to light another match. Susan pulled her sweater a little closer, and then huddled down beside Laura.

"Can I have one?"

Laura looked over, and smiled, her white teeth dazzling unnaturally in the chill of that October afternoon. She pulled out another cigarette and handed it to Susan. She thought back to those afternoons with Delia, and of how times had changed.

"I didn't know you smoked either."

Laura lit Susan's cigarette, and then her own, and they both took the first, awesome drag of those long-forbidden cigarettes, and sighed, and then began to giggle.

"Look at us, like a couple of schoolgirls behind the outhouse."

"The outhouse?"

"Well, some building or other. That just sprang to mind."

Susan looked at the six cans of paint thinner in Laura's cart.

"Doing some house cleaning?" she asked dryly, as she took another drag.

Laura didn't answer right away, and paused to flick some ash onto the concrete at her feet. She cleared her throat a few times.

"Just loading up on a few supplies. Brian painted the whole house last year and the garage is full of old paint cans and spills and brushes. You know, you get the supplies in, you get the job done."

"Uh huh. How is Brian anyway? Still drawing up financial plans for the collected wealth of Chisholm? In between dry-cleaning their stuffed shirts."

Susan laughed at her own little joke but Laura remained silent.

"Laura? Is everything okay?"

The events of the day rose up in Laura's throat like bile but wouldn't come out in words.

"I've been thinking about this franchise stuff for Twisted. Got me kind of preoccupied."

They puffed away quietly for a while, watching people come in and go out of Home Hardware, listening to the jingle bell clinking and rattling of their carts on the pavement.

Laura stared ahead as shoppers dashed in and out, intent on reaching their cars and their trunks and their respective houses, supplies in hand, lives under control.

"Do you ever wonder about where your life would have gone if you hadn't married Henry?" Laura didn't look at Susan as she asked this; she continued looking ahead, as if into a crystal ball where another future hung suspended like a fly trapped in amber.

"I used to think about it all the time. Then I stopped. It was like being trapped on this Lazy Susan going round and round and every time I thought I'd jump off I got nervous and stayed put."

"God, we're pathetic, aren't we?'

Susan, who had always thought that Laura and Brian were made for each other, didn't quite know what to make of the question.

"Laura, did something happen?

"I'm going to have to go. I'll catch up with you later." Laura stood up abruptly and dumped the cigarettes on Susan's lap. "Here, have these. Keep you out of mischief."

That night at dinner, if Brian didn't know better, he'd have thought Laura was stoned. Everything looked normal, but something wasn't right. Everything Laura did was exactly the same, the same white crockery bowls filled with steaming food brought in from the kitchen, the table laid out the same way, cut up vegetables for the children, her small yellow apron designed with bee appliqués tied the same way around her small waist, and Brian had to admit he'd had fantasies of her wearing that apron and nothing else. She had unpacked the children's lunches and put the blue ice-gel packs back in the freezer and cleaned out the tiny Rubbermaid containers that had held cut up fruit and homemade puddings. He always loved family dinners, the children gathered round, the bustle of serving spoons and plates passed from one to another. He liked the knowledge he was the head of this busy noisy little family. But Laura's eyes were curiously bright, alert, shining.

"How was your sister today?'

Laura forked a solitary pea from her plate.

"Oh, fine, you know, same as ever."

"And the kids, they doing all right?"

Laura poked a second one.

"Great, great. Alex got a scholarship to study in Halifax."

Every time Laura poked her fork into a pea the fork scraped the china plate and made a sound that caused him to wince.

"Laura, why are you eating those peas like that?"

The children giggled and poked each other. The youngest one tried putting a pea up his nose.

"Oh, I don't know. Makes a change, I guess."

Laura said the last line with considerable emphasis. Brian forged on.

"Did you try out the washer yet?"

"Haven't had time. More potatoes?" Laura smiled vacuously.

"Thanks. Well, it'll be good to get those clothes washed finally. I think I've been wearing the same pants now for days."

There was more scraping and prodding of peas. Brian suddenly realized Laura wasn't actually eating her peas, but lining them up in a circle around a blob of mashed potatoes. She raised her fork to her cheek, and then gestured with it to her eldest child.

"Gasoline, butane, or propane. What do you call these, Robert?"

At twelve, Robert was a good student, especially in science, like his mother.

"Complex hydrocarbons."

"Right, good, good. And why do we call them that?"

"They have lots of carbon in them."

"Right again. High carbon and hydrogen content. And what does that mean?"

It didn't occur to Brian that this was a rather odd conversation, because Laura had a habit of quizzing her children about schoolwork at dinner. It was the only time they sat still long enough to really be asked anything. So Brian continued to eat his dinner, combining stuffed pork roast with lumps of potato and peas on his fork, munching contentedly.

"They burn like crazy!" piped up the younger one, Michael, who was ten, and smart, and had a certain way with words. "Major combustion!"

"Exactly. Major combustion."

"Which is why we don't go near matches and lighters or keep greasy rags around the house, right?" Brian chimed in importantly, seeing a pedagogical opportunity and a chance to sound parental. "Correct?"

"Correct," they all answered together, and Brian smiled to himself, thinking he'd scored a point and picturing Laura naked again except for the yellow apron. He wondered what he'd been thinking having that fling with Tabitha. But now it was over, there was no harm done. It must have been a temporary lapse of judgment, he thought again, she'd cast some kind of witchy spell on him. It wasn't his fault. This is where he wanted to be, at the head of his family, bringing home the bacon and all that, helping with the dishes after supper and taking the kids apple picking in the fall, sledding in the winter, helping with their homework. And making love to his wife, his sweet wonderful wife, who at that moment was busily calculating the molecular activity needed to keep a fire burning, and wondering how many matches it would take to ignite an oily rag, and deciding how many rags she would need to circle the house, like a band of Indians round an unsuspecting stagecoach.

A Thousand Uses for Ashes

"You may be tempted, dear reader, to throw out those ashes from the fireplace, throw them out with the stale breadcrusts and the empty tuna tins, but there is a higher purpose for those greying and charred remains. Let me enlighten you:

— take a pronged tool, such as a fork, and work the ashes in around your blueberry bushes, for a delightful mulch;

— is your soil a trifle short on potash? Incorporate your ashes! (well, not yours, exactly, dear reader, you know what I mean!);

— are grandmother's candlesticks looking a wee bit dull? Silver polish, oh enlightened readers, use those ashes to polish your silver!;

— repell slugs, snails, unwanted lovers and other household pests!"

From *Everyman's Guide to the Modern Universe and Household Management*, Nathaniel P. Speck, Professor of Medieval History, St Simons University, Chisholm, Nova Scotia

Nine

It was a long, treacherous slide, but once it had begun, there was no turning back. Tabitha tried to deal with her emotions by delving into the bottomless pit of reorganization. First the bedroom cupboard. This had to go. This. That. Skirts, blouses, jackets, jeans flung out behind her like kites in the wind. It was the most restorative tonic she knew. Brian had turned out to be just like any other man – hardly the passionate soulmate she was looking for! Tabitha had been little more than a diversion! Hardly the stuff of which harmonious attraction was made! So let him stay there, she fumed, in his puny self-satisfied little household.

And with every outfit she tossed behind her went some pointless seduction, this man, that man, one bed, then another, so that by the end, surrounded by a slumping mass of tangled fabrics, buttons, zippers, and drawstrings, she felt a kind of shallow catharsis. She went on to other rooms, lining up the soup tins in the cupboard, from large to small, alphabetizing the books on the shelf, and folding each towel, dishcloth and facecloth so that the corners were perfect. She lined up sheets of paper in the drawer, rolled her socks into neat little balls and arranged them in a shoe box, turned all the coloured pencils right side up and threw out those whose height and size threw off the jagged symmetry of the jar where she kept them, coloured leads up, pointed, and all precisely sharpened to the same acute angle.

The business with Brian had transformed her thwarted energies into a bustling mass of precision and neatness. She had been naïve, ridiculous, a fool. Tabitha stuffed the piles of rejected clothes into a large green garbage bag. She had been used again, a brief diversion from the stifling monotony of married life, and then she had been tossed, again, as surely as an old Kleenex. Tabitha had thrown herself at him, it was true, but she intended to offer him everything, all of her ideas, Fourier's theories, the chance to be part of Harmony, a pioneer of a new social order. But Brian had pressed the pause button on sex. Yes, she intended that too, but as part of an amorous, blissful natural salute to one's inevitable sensuality, not the amateurish groping she had experienced with Brian. Tabitha didn't like to admit it, but jumping into bed was always meant to be a doorway into closeness, into permanence. Of course it never was, and she didn't seem to learn. But the contentment sex used to provide was not only shallow, but fast fading. It occurred to Tabitha that getting older was like a long emotional striptease, as each form of solace got peeled off and finally there you were, left naked, stripped bare of everything you ever had to help you get through.

Fourier's words began seeping up through the tunnels of her mind. "Lost, in the black night, let us begin by seeking a more dependable guiding light than the so-called reason that has led us astray." Yes, yes, where is the light in the wilderness? She used to think it was love, in fact Fourier had persuaded her it was love, but where had love left her? Yet Fourier had convinced her once it was the only passion that reflected the divine spirit. Paul's face kept drifting in front of her but she steered herself into another fervent bustle of activity rather than face up to what she had lost. She pulled open the right-hand drawer of her desk.

And began her inventory:

1. twelve miniature audio cassettes for a tape recorder she no longer owned
2. four dollars worth of Canadian Tire money she never had with her when she went there
3. six glasses cases, all empty
4. her immunization record from when she was six
5. about 200 address stickers from charities which she never supported, festooned with various butterflies, puppies, and sunsets
6. pens that no longer worked
7. dried up glue sticks
8. old shopping lists
9. a macramé pencil case (!)
10. various organizational office-supply kits, with blank pads and unfilled binders
11. a tampon
12. her astrological forecast from 1988, which Paul had folded into an origami frog.

She had forgotten about that frog, but now every detail of its creation came tumbling back. They had been at Wu Fats, sharing a glass of bubble tea and reading over the Chinese horoscope printed out on the placemat. It was the year of the dog (I'll say, she thought). The forecast hadn't been good, and Paul, in an effort to cheer her up, had begun the mesmerizing process of folding up the paper until it was no longer a prediction of financial and personal ruin but a playful frog that could hop from plate to plate with the tap of a finger on its tail. Paul had been able to transform everything, ceilings into constellations, placemats into creatures, Tabitha into the girl who was wanted. She gave it a little tap with her finger and it hopped once across her desk and fell over the side. She slid down on the floor beside it, and began ripping it into little pieces, the shredding gathering momentum as she went along. Why couldn't he have stayed? Why couldn't he have loved her back? Finally the mangled frog lay at her feet, a black and white confetti of regret. Tabitha leaned her head back against the desk, and a deep slumber began to take over.

In her dream Tabitha floated like a tiny bubble inside a larger bubble. She tried to focus, but the landscape kept shifting. Inside, then out, inside, then out, she floated, popped and then disappeared. Then suddenly she was lifted from a suburban backyard wedding, plucked from the arms of some faceless bridegroom, by a man in white. Tabitha moved radiantly throughout the air, her white gauze robe furling and unfurling in the breeze. The man who had rescued her was Paul, of course, but then pop! She was back outside again, peering in through a film of shiny stuff like liquid Glad Wrap. She had to focus more, surely that was the way to do it.

It took some doing, but soon she was back. Paul was slowly lifting away the layers of white gauze and kissing every little patch of skin that appeared. Tabitha was about to settle into the dream when a large mushroom cloud of a list began to obliterate her dreamy romance. Even in her sleep, she was unable to prevent the formation of lists, it was like mould growing in the back of the fridge. Reasons why it would never have worked with Paul:

He was intimidated by my intelligence.
He was too good looking.
He was cheap.

Paul and Tabitha's lips moved towards each other and remained suspended at the same time, the way that something you want so badly is always best when left in its anticipated state. But the list returned, as if printed out on a long scroll:

He refused to let me use a fork at Wu Fats.
Glow in the dark stars – come on, grow up.
He wanted to be a poet, for Christ sake.

He spent his spare time chiselling out arrowheads from rocks. Duh.

Tabitha crept back inside her dream bubble. Paul and a flock of people who appeared to be angels were now in the centre of a giant field, holding hands and chanting. Tabitha began chanting idly until a final entry to the list jolted her awake.

He could poison you with the right mushroom.

Tabitha woke up with a start, her neck stiff from leaning awkwardly in sleep against the hard wooden desk. There was a weird acrid smell in the air, and it looked as though her house was filling up with smoke. She lifted herself from the floor, and the crumbled remnants of Paul's workmanship fell from her lap, showering down onto the carpet. For some reason, a picture of a mushroom popped into her head, and she tried to recall what she had been dreaming about. Paul was there, she knew that from the ache of longing she always felt when she woke up from one of those dreams, the ones where all the past gets forgotten and everything is forgiven and the man you really loved mysteriously appears back in your life and you get to start all over again.

But there was no time to be wistful. There was smoke, and the small crackling sounds of sticks being snapped in half. Her house was on fire! Tabitha grabbed the laptop from her desk, pulled the cord from the wall, and charged towards the back door. She banged it open with her foot, lunged over her porch, and leaped through the back yard. She had just got out in time. She stopped, turned around, and watched as her house, the little pale blue wooden bungalow, began to burn. At some point, and she didn't know why, the fire department arrived, then all of her neighbours. She took in the red truck, the incredible sky-high whoosh of the water jets, the smoke, the flames, the smell. But as she stood there, as the voices of consolation and disbelief whirled around her, Tabitha felt herself sharpening, centring, closing in on herself so that finally there was no one else around. She looked for Rosa in the patterns of smoke that poured from the windows, but Tabitha was completely alone, even as she was whisked off to a neighbour's house for a jolt of brandy and offers of upstairs rooms, basement apartments, and pull-out sofas. Alone as the firemen questioned her about how the fire could have started. Alone, as Brian and Laura joined the crowd of shocked and sympathetic onlookers, and as the talk of arson began seeping through the huddle, as they shook their heads and wondered how this could have happened on their quiet little street, a street where no one ever had anything bad to say against anyone.

As she sat nursing her Scotch, she was glad she didn't have to say anything, or be polite, or even respond to direct questions. From this perfect, still centre of being alone, Tabitha found the resolve and the will first to get herself away from the well-intentioned neighbours to a motel, the Chisholm Arms. Here she could sleep on calm white anonymous sheets, and not have anyone peering over at her, pointing, trying to figure out what to say, sticking her under the microscope of curiosity masking itself as concern.

The Chisholm Arms was situated at the edge of the Sobeys parking lot, a once-turquoise building that had now faded into a colour impossible to describe except as non-descript. There were twelve rooms upstairs and twelve rooms downstairs; some of the lower doors looked as though someone may have tried to kick them in and these had a second set of locks inside. The rooms were vaguely turquoise too, with chenille bedspreads and Day-Glo art on the walls, a kind of neon seashore. Black and white televisions loomed from the corners. The rooms smelled like stale cigarettes and mould, that peculiar musty damp that breeds bacteria and the growth of all things unhealthy and furtive. There were no phones in the rooms, however, so Tabitha walked outside to the pay phone she had spotted next to the motel office. Even the receiver smelled like cigarette smoke, body odour and musty basements, and Tabitha held it as far away from her face as she could while still being heard.

"Hello. Speck Residence."

"Nathaniel, it's Tabitha. From the university."

There was a silence, and then an almost audible question mark.

"Tabitha?"

"Yes, have you seen the smoke?"

"Smoke? I've been in my study working. I haven't seen anything."

"Someone set my house on fire. I wasn't supposed to be there, I had a faculty meeting, but I'm lucky to be alive."

"Good God! I'm going to go to my window and look out. Hang on."

"No, wait, Nathaniel, don't go. I mean, there's something I need to ask you."

Tabitha took a deep breath, and peered down the walkway of the Chisholm Arms Motel, each door lined up at a polite distance from the other, cars lined up like a drive-in movie out front, the fake and faded red geraniums huddled and straggling in the window boxes outside every room. She let the breath go, and the words escape.

"Nathaniel, I'll need a place to stay for a while, and I was wondering if I could stay with you."

There was more silence, and Tabitha turned the other way, to the office, where a young couple with a bickering child was emerging from a Volvo station wagon, the three of them looking crumpled and cranky from a long drive, the prospect of the motel room an unexpected bliss.

"I'd cover all my costs, of course, pay for my food."

Nathaniel hadn't mentioned about Fiona to Tabitha, and while there wasn't anything to hide, the fact of his not mentioning it suddenly took on more importance than it should have. He scrambled to get the information out in the right way, and wondered how he would manage with two women in his house.

"Well, look, there is a small problem."

As Nathaniel was talking, Bill ambled over and began licking Nathaniel's bare toes, which were sticking out of a hole in his slipper. In trying to kick him away he dropped the phone with a clang and accidentally banged the receiver with his elbow, severing the connection. Tabitha heard an abrupt click, and then the desolate monotony of the dial tone. "A small problem," she had heard, and that was enough. She decided not to call back. She knew he was only trying to be polite, while at the same time saying no, and she walked with highly dejected footsteps along the concrete path back to Room 117. What could she have been thinking? She and Nathaniel barely knew each other. It was too much to ask to stay there. She turned the key in the door and stepped inside. A light rain had started. Without bothering to turn on the lights, she flopped down on the bed and pulled the pale green chenille bedspread up to her chin. There was a small stain near the bottom of it, coffee or blood. She didn't much care.

Nathaniel was beside himself. He didn't even know where Tabitha was calling from. He didn't know how to reach her. A mesmerizing rain was falling by now, hard and relentless. Fiona was in the laundry room, ironing some of his shirts, and as he walked in a pleasant, sunny-day outdoorsy smell reached his nose. Fiona was gaily spraying the shirts with an aerosol can covered in blue sky and clouds.

"Fiona. Something terrible's happened. A fire."

She looked up from the ironing board.

"A fire! Where?"

"In town. A friend of mine."

"Is he all right? Good God, don't tell me…"

"No, no. She, actually. She's fine. But she just called me. She needs somewhere to stay, and I accidentally cut her off, and I don't know where she's calling from, and I need to get back…"

Fiona unplugged the iron and took Nathaniel by the elbow and into the living room.

"You've got one of those fancy fucking phones, Nathaniel, you can get the number by dialling star 69."

"Really?"

Fiona nodded and a huge grin came over Nathaniel's face. He thought about how apprehensive he had been when Fiona came to stay, and how well it had worked out, really, although she wasn't going to stay there forever, was she.

Nathaniel dialled star 69 and to his surprise the number was announced to him by the flat and toneless voice of the automated operator. He dialled it with his large hands and waited as the phone rang into the night. Such a lonely sound, Nathaniel decided, so insistent and hopeful, even as no one answered. He put the phone down, and dialled again.

"Nathaniel, for fuck's sake, you don't need to dial again, just press redial."

By the fifth set of rings, the sound of the payphone ringing into the bleak night had got the attention of the motel manager, who was still processing the couple with the screaming child, now banging on the bell for service until he took it away from him and put it behind the cash. Seizing an opportunity to get away from the belligerent child for a moment, he grabbed his yellow mac, flipped up the hood and dashed out to the payphone in the rain.

"Hello. Chisholm Arms Motel. Can I help you?"

"Oh, thank God, this is Nathaniel Speck, Professor of Medieval Literature at St Simons."

"Professor. What can I do for you?"

"Someone called me from there a few moments ago. Tabitha Black. I need to get in touch with her."

"Oh, she's here all right. House burned down in a fire, you know."

"Yes, yes, that's why I need to speak with her."

"She's in Room 117. I don't see any lights on down there. Maybe she's asleep."

"Oh, don't wake her up. Thanks. Look, perhaps I'll just come down there." He paused. "And perhaps I'll have the chance to try out your establishment sometime." The way Nathaniel said establishment made it seem less seedy than it really was, and the man pumped up with pride at the multi-syllabic splendour of it. Nathaniel simply felt he owed the man something for answering the phone.

"Anytime, professor."

Nathaniel drove his minivan in the driving rain to the Chisholm Arms, the rain now falling so hard he was almost unable to see the road ahead. He had the windshield wipers set at frantic but it was still touch and go – was that the road or the curb? The sidewalk or a ditch?

It was with considerable relief that he reached the motel, and pulled up beside the office. In his haste to get there he hadn't packed an umbrella or even a rain jacket, and he got soaked just running from the car to Tabitha's room. He banged on the door, and stood, dripping, waiting for Tabitha to open it. Finally he sensed movement from behind the locked door. Tabitha opened it onto the darkness and the rain, and was surprised to see Nathaniel standing there, his matted hair now plastered flat to his head, his tweed jacket a soggy, sodden disaster. As she looked down, she realized he had forgotten to put on his shoes, and protruding from his old slippers his toes were perfectly bare, shining like white beacons in the storm.

"We got cut off. I didn't want you to think…"

Tabitha reached out for Nathaniel's arm and pulled him inside the dry haven of her room. He huddled by the door, creating a puddle as he stood, still stumbling through some kind of explanation for why she had been cut off. Tabitha wasn't really listening – she pulled all the thin and faintly grey towels from the bathroom and threw them to Nathaniel, who began rubbing his head with a facecloth that had seen better days. Finally she began to hear the low and resonant honey of his voice.

"It was that damn dog. I'm so sorry Tabitha. All I was about to say was that one of my spare rooms is already taken up. My cousin, Fiona, is staying." He stopped rubbing his head for a moment. "But just for a while."

Tabitha could hear the rain falling on the flat roof above her. She suddenly felt embarrassed that she had even called Nathaniel. And how presumptuous was she! Thinking that Nathaniel had no one in the world and would be the logical person on whose floor to camp out until she could find her own place. And here he was! A cousin visiting! A Fiona!

"Tabitha, you would be most welcome to stay with me. My humble home is yours for as long as you need."

Tabitha recognized in the syntax of Nathaniel's invitation the same archaic gentlemanliness she had uncovered in his letters to Rashida. She softened, relaxed.

"Oh, thank God. I thought I'd end up at some neighbours. I thought I'd become that weird lady from down the street living upstairs. 'She's from away, you know."

Nathaniel grinned, and Tabitha grinned, the first time since she'd fled her house.

"You'd best get out of those wet clothes, Nathaniel, or you'll get sick."

"I've got to get back. Storms make Fiona nervous."

Nathaniel handed her the pile of thin, and now sopping towels, and turned back out into the storm. Tabitha watched him as he disappeared into the protection of his minivan, saw his large dark shape at the wheel, like a bear. Then she closed the door, and dumped the towels into the bathtub. She didn't have the energy to hang them up. She'd call the manager in the morning for new towels, have a hot shower, eat a hot breakfast, and head over to Nathaniel's. By tomorrow, she was sure, the storm would have cleared, and her head along with it. She crept back into the bed, closed her eyes, and dreamed of grasshoppers chewing through electrical wires, their charred little bodies piling up like blackened clothes pegs inside walls, fires starting throughout Chisholm, people shaking their heads and muttering – it was the hoppers, you know, the hoppers that did it.

The next day dawned bright as a flashlight, and Nathaniel was up earlier than usual, tearing open the curtains and then immediately regretting it, as the daylight revealed with cruel accuracy how comfortably domestic Nathaniel's life with Fiona had actually become. Nathaniel hadn't owned a television until Fiona arrived, and yet there it now stood, its faceless screen covered in a thin dust, in the centre of the large picture window, its single unblinking eye turned away from the mysteries of Bluejacket Bay and facing directly into the twin comfy chairs that stared right back, their cushions wrinkled into the shapes of Nathaniel and Fiona. Across the arm of one of the chairs rested a holder, a limply stuffed daschund, its tail made into a neat little pocket perfectly sized to the remote. Fiona's knitting sat in a basket beside her chair, and beside that was a cup of forgotten tea, a small white ring of scum forming on the surface. Beside Nathaniel's chair was a pile of *Scientific American* journals, mostly unread, as Nathaniel found himself almost completely unable to concentrate with the television on. Settled deep into the cracks of this blissful scene were puffs of popcorn spilled from the bowl, cookie crumbs, cracker ends, solidified cheese curls and the odd hairpin. And into the midst of this came Bill, who jumped up on Nathaniel's chair, circled three times and sniffed his tail, then settled into one corner for a morning nap.

Nathaniel was distraught. Just then Fiona came into the room, her eyes still soft from sleep and her hair transformed from the night into a wild, pre-brush fuzz.

"What are you doing up so early?"

"Fiona, I have an announcement."

In her groggy state, Fiona thought Nathaniel was about to finally kick her out of the house, and she immediately fell into a litany of self-criticism – why hadn't she made plans herself, got things organized? Why hadn't she tried to find a place to live? She rubbed her sleepy eyes and felt ridiculous. Why hadn't she made the first move, taken charge? Instead she was going to have to endure this humiliation.

"We're going to have a guest."

Fiona stopped rubbing her eyes and looked up in surprise.

"A guest?"

"Yes. The woman whose house burned down? I offered her the room at the back. She's got nowhere else to go. I was going to tell you last night, but you were asleep when I got back."

Fiona was rapidly trying to process the information that Nathaniel was giving her, but without her first cup of tea it wasn't really registering. Nathaniel was busily trying to move the television to a less conspicuous spot, but the cable had it pinned to the floor where it stood, and when he pulled the connection from the back of the set the wire shot back and down the hole and disappeared.

"Well, there goes the Discovery fucking Channel," Fiona said loudly, and went off to the kitchen to make tea. "You'd think we were expecting the Queen." she said to herself, softly, so Nathaniel couldn't hear. Not that he would have heard anyway, he was too busy, straightening out cushions, flicking crumbs to the floor so he could vacuum them up, clattering into the kitchen with a leaning tower of plates and cups. He found himself eyeing the books on the shelf, selecting just the right one to display beside his chair. Perhaps *A Discussion of Marriage and Morals in the Middle Ages*, or *Hildegard's Scivias*, in its original German, of course.

Bill was still sitting on the chair, watching Nathaniel going to and fro like someone in a tennis match. It was pleasing, and so familiar, this level of frenetic activity, at least if you were a dog. Bill recognized that wonderful heat you feel sniffing out and digging up a bone, your paws like crazed shovels and the dirt going every which way.

But it was not pleasing to Fiona, who stood thinking as the steam rose from the kettle and began its slow process of eating away at the wood of the cupboards. She had to admit she was becoming used to life with Nathaniel, and that in some small part of her brain she thought it might go on forever. But now there was someone else coming, and she knew deep in the pit of her little rounded stomach that everything would change. The cozy, sexless, no-demands relationship they had developed was teetering on the edge of extinction. There was nothing she could do. She poured her tea, and was about to pour Nathaniel's, when he appeared in the doorway with her knitting basket, gesturing wildly at the broom closet for somewhere to put it, and she changed her mind.

Coping with Unexpected Guests

   "The best thing to do with unexpected guests is to let them know that you, and you alone, are master of the household, and they must be obedient to your dictates. Master, chief cook, ruler of your household. Guests must assume a subservient role, and you must see to it that they do! Otherwise guests can end up staying too long and crowding the proverbial welcome mat, like bacteria. Avoid the use of foul language, of course, but if they seem to be overstepping their bounds, tell them, and do not mince your words, that they must depart. Forthwith!"

   From *Everyman's Guide to the Modern Universe and Household Management*, Nathaniel P. Speck, Professor of Medieval History, St Simons University, Chisholm, Nova Scotia

Ten

Tabitha hadn't seen Laura since the afternoon she had spotted her in Tim Hortons talking to herself, so she wasn't sure she even recognized her when her face appeared from the shadows of the murky TV screen in Room 117 of the Chisholm Arms Motel. But sure enough, there she was, on the local cable station! The make-up people had done a number on her, of course, and her hair now hung in a stylish bob, swept slightly to one side. She was also wearing a fashionable pantsuit and high heels. Tabitha searched around the wreckage of her sheets for the remote control to turn up the volume.

"Now, where is it you said you come from?" The reporter flashed his toothiest smile at the audience, and Laura smiled too.

"It's a little town called Fallon. Right next door to Chisholm. Population: five hundred. Restaurants: one, if you count the Tim Hortons."

"A hot bed of social activism, no doubt!" The reporter laughed.

"Well, it was actually at a Tim Hortons that I came up with the idea of turning Twisted into a franchise operation. Sitting there with my fritter."

The young man who was interviewing Laura looked positively enchanted with her. It was just the kind of feel-good story their researchers went after, and Laura was so, well, earnest.

"But here's what I want to ask you. Now, how did you come up with this idea in the first place? I mean, really, you're a frog researcher." Laura appeared to wince at this moniker. "You have no background in psychology, or even business, for that matter, and you've come up with a corporate miracle – an enterprise that is estimated to be worth millions in the next two years. Why, you'll be bigger than Doctor Phil!"

Tabitha looked at her watch. Quarter past four. She wondered how long this gushing adoration would go on. The program had three quarters of an hour left. She could hardly believe Laura had got herself on television.

"Well, the idea is so simple, so obvious. But it had been right in front of me the whole time. I just couldn't see it. You know when you sleep, and all that subconscious stuff comes rising up to the surface, and you can't do anything about it, because you're asleep, well, that's the place to explore to find out what's really going on."

The young man was looking down at his notes. "Disparity of sheets."

"That's how I describe it. Of course, there is also companion-ability of sheets. The ideal relationship. And dealing with flannel: what does it say about your sexual preferences?"

The reporter was nodding excitedly. "These sound a lot like chapter headings for a book."

Laura turned towards the camera. She seemed to have instinctive media savvy. "Exactly. I'm writing it now. And everyone who orders a Twisted franchise kit will receive a free copy, absolutely free, just for ordering one."

"Now Laura, I've got to ask you. When you discovered this method of analyzing relationships, I imagine the first one you tried it out on was your own. Tell me, do you suffer from disparity of sheets in your marriage bed?"

Laura leaned forward, tucking a stray lock of hair behind her ears. "As a journalist, you must understand that the secret of any business like mine is absolute and complete confidentiality."

The reporter winked at the audience.

"You mean you'll never tell."

"Exactly."

Tabitha flopped back on the bed and turned off the sound. She was still trying to reconcile the Laura she had met just a few months ago with the media maven on her TV screen. Yet another side to her personality! Just as Tabitha had been completely wrong in her theories about Brian, it looked as if she had been wrong about Laura too. It was unsettling, having everything turned upside down this way, no longer able to trust herself. Yet even as she felt the isolation of constant doubt, she began to realize that in a strange and life-affirming twist, the fire had been exactly what she needed. Forget about closets or new agenda books or even the start of the academic term. This was rebirth on a whole new scale. Fire had been the great purifier, the ultimate list maker. Now she would be forced to set up Harmony for real, not just play about with the theory at a safe and comfortable distance. Nathaniel's place would be a temporary shelter while she worked things out with the architects. Perhaps once it was built, the right occupants might hear the signal and flock. The first inhabitants of Harmony were probably closer than she even realized. She pulled herself up awkwardly from the bed and went into the bathroom to run the shower, get herself dressed, and head for Nathaniel's.

As she turned into the driveway of his house, the brand new clothes in their plastic bags in the back seat seemed possessed of their own life, anxious to begin, restless with their tags and washing instructions and just-bought sheen. Her laptop lay beside them, with all of her notes on Fourier, her class outlines, lecture notes, essay topics and exams, her teaching schedule, all her financial information. In another bag was a bright red toothbrush, a spanking new cosmetic bag filled with fresh makeup, toothpaste, floss, cotton pads, shampoo, conditioner, a hairbrush made with real sable bristles from France.

She stepped out of the car and smelled the salt sea tang of the air, mixed with woodsmoke from the fireplace. She looked over the bay, where the water was the colour of tarnished pewter and cold, cold, cold, for winter was now definitely on its way.

The town was buzzing with talk of the record-setting winter storm approaching from the west, and Tabitha remembered that's usually how winter started in Chisholm. A sudden thumping storm, and the next day instant winter, the ground covered in two feet of snow, the windows frozen, and invariably one or two accidents on the highway in from Halifax. But she wouldn't have to face this storm alone. She knocked.

The door swung open and Fiona surveyed the unlikely creature who stood there. Tabitha, thin as a reed, wearing pale blue jeans and a bright yellow mac, her black hair burnished and shiny like the surface of a still pond. Fiona recalled her manners and ushered her in.

"I'm Fiona. You must be the guest."

The word "guest" had an edge in it, the way Fiona said it.

"Hello. I'm Tabitha Black. It's good to meet you."

Fiona shut the door behind her and offered to take her coat. For a moment she felt like the maid, and then realized she was probably being silly, and then looked over at Tabitha and thought the same again, and pointed to the row of hooks on the wall so Tabitha could hang it herself. But then she found herself offering Tabitha a cup of tea. Nathaniel had gone shopping for extra food, and Fiona was on her own. With the guest.

"Tea would be good."

Tabitha followed Fiona into the kitchen, noting as she did some of the changes that had taken place in Nathaniel's house since the last time she was there. She hadn't remembered curtains, frilly pillow shams, or fake geraniums in pots along the top of the bookcase. The kitchen was even more of a revelation, stocked with canisters, aprons hanging on hooks (his and hers?) and a decorative plastic bottle for dish detergent shaped like a woman, a blue ribbon tied round her waist.

"I see you've made a few changes around here."

Fiona was surprised to hear that Tabitha had been here before, but tried not to let it show.

"A few, yes. It was so plain when I got here. No character."

Tabitha nodded, and tried to sum up the relationship between Nathaniel and Fiona.

"So, you're Nathaniel's cousin."

Fiona rattled some teacups from the back of the cupboard and tipped ginger biscuits onto a plate. She puffed up her hair a little, which had grown since the terrible razor cut, and smoothed down her skirt, a wonderful paisley creation she had bought on a whim once in Halifax. She'd taken some extra care with herself that day, and she didn't want it to go unnoticed.

"Fourth cousin, twice removed, or some such thing. Course we've got lots of cousins, our family, but we don't see most of them. Tell me about the fire."

Fiona wanted to steer the conversation away from herself. She didn't want to be probed or examined under the microscope by the guest. Guest popped into her mind with a capital G.

"I don't know what the hell happened. I've got to phone the insurance people this morning. I suppose at some point I'm going to have to go over and sort it out. But to tell you the truth, I'm not really that anxious to go back there."

On some level Fiona wanted to bond with Tabitha. After all, she'd wanted to leave something behind too. But as soon as she got the urge to spill out her own story, something held her back, and the facts of her life with Dick got trapped in her throat like breadcrumbs. If she had to follow their trail back down she'd have to admit she'd been a fool.

Fiona gobbled down two ginger creams to every one of Tabitha's, and wished Nathaniel would get back soon so she could excuse herself and lie down or hang up laundry or do anything but be in the same room as the two of them. She'd have to eventually, of course, but she wasn't ready yet. Before Tabitha arrived, Fiona had felt perfectly in charge, she was the woman of the house, the one who got there first. But she hadn't been expecting this. Tabitha had to be ten years younger than Fiona. And weren't all academic women frumps and bespectacled, with unkempt hair and fingers gnarled from their grip on pens, their faces roadmaps of wrinkles from all that thinking? She'd been expecting a female version of Nathaniel. And what did she get? Fucking Mata Hari.

"I don't know much about Nathaniel really, or his family. I didn't even know he had so many relatives."

You knew him well enough to fucking invite yourself over, though didn't you, Fiona thought.

"Nathaniel's a dear man. I've known him since he was a child." Fiona turned to Tabitha and fixed her with a look similar to the kind people who wear glasses have perfected, peering over the tops of the rims and raising their eyebrows, except that Fiona didn't wear glasses and her eyebrows were so tweezed they were almost invisible, so that instead of looking formidable, she looked demented. "Most people don't understand him."

By most people, Fiona meant Tabitha. But Tabitha, having been privy to the unabashedly romantic correspondence between Nathaniel and Rashida, felt herself to understand Nathaniel in a way she was sure Fiona could never do.

"I'm not sure what you mean." Tabitha replied.

Fiona took a long sip from her tea and sighed. She looked up, and then down at the floor, and then back up at the ceiling again.

"How can I put it. Nathaniel isn't, well, he isn't your typical man now is he?"

Tabitha snorted with laughter.

"You mean weak, easily seduced, and fundamentally ignorant of what it means to love someone?" she replied, unaware of how aptly she was describing herself.

Fiona had been trying really hard, ever since Tabitha arrived, not to swear, but the bang-on quality of the description uttered from Tabitha's lips was just too good an opportunity to pass up.

"Holy fuck, are you sure you've never met my husband?"

Just then they heard the front door slam open, and then slam shut, and Nathaniel appeared at the kitchen door, shopping bags piled in both arms, his hair curiously askew from the wind that he seemed to stir up entirely on his own when he walked.

"Ah, good, I see you two have met. Fiona, could you take these for me?"

Fiona didn't see why she should take them, and remained motionless by the sink. Tabitha stepped into the breach and took them. She began pulling out cans and packets from the bags and wondering how Nathaniel had made his selection. There were several cans of cream corn, some animal crackers, packets of instant noodles, tinned tomato paste, pepperoni sticks, instant pudding, 100 percent rye bread (thank God there was something there to eat), instant coffee, whole milk, frozen pink lemonade and a plastic bag filled with limes and lemons.

"I'm sure we can whip together some dinner out of that, eh?"

He wandered out of the room, tripped over Bill and cursed. Fiona put down her cup.

"I knew I should have made him a list. I usually do."

Tabitha began to wonder if she had done the right thing descending on Nathaniel's doorstep.

And Fiona wasn't doing much to make her feel welcome. But as she was calculating just how long she might have to stay there, an ethereal sound floated in from the living room, the sound of an angel singing surely, a distant and pure voice so perfectly registered that it could only be from heaven.

Tabitha picked up her teacup and walked into the living room, where Nathaniel was picking through his collection of medieval music CDs.

"What is that heavenly music? I've never heard anything like it!"

Fiona, chopping up pepperoni sticks in the kitchen, could hear the conversation going on in the living room, and under her breath she imitated Tabitha in a high-pitched sing song. "What is that heavenly fucking music, oh Nathaniel, I've never heard anything like it, oh, oh."

"I knew you would appreciate it. "Nathaniel held out the CD case for Tabitha to look at. "Sarband. They match European music to medieval Islamic and Jewish music. Fascinating."

"Occident meets orient – that sort of thing."

"That's it. That's it exactly."

The sweet and seductive sound of a single female voice chanting, punctuated every few seconds with only the gentle peal of a distant bell, was entrancing, mesmerizing. Tabitha fell back in Fiona's chair, spellbound.

Fiona poked her head around the corner.

"Who wants pink lemonade?"

But neither of them heard her, all swept up in the music as they were.

"Pink fucking lemonade anyone?" Fiona shouted, and caught their attention.

"Lovely, that would be lovely," they both said at once, and laughed.

Fiona returned to the kitchen and wondered if there were any poisons in the house. But then she thought better of it. After all, she thought, someone's just tried to burn her house down. Give the girl a break.

It was a strange sight, Fiona, Nathaniel and Tabitha lined up like the pots on the bookcase, pepperoni sandwiches and lemonade set out before them on TV tables, the three of them facing towards the Bay. Bill was curled up at Nathaniel's feet, Tabitha was wrapped in the grey afghan, and Fiona was trying to figure out just what life would be like with Tabitha being there. She called Bill over to her, rubbing her thumb and her index finger together, their secret signal. Bill trotted over, and collapsed at Fiona's feet. She had been around long enough to know that something would have to give; she just wasn't sure what, or who.

The Saving Grace of Marriage

"A plague on both sexes was how one nineteenth-century philosopher described marriage, but gentle readers, do not go there. Despite rumours to the contrary, marriage can be the ultimate, life-sustaining force in a perilous world. Like the savage beasts in the field, you must be loving and friendly with those who feed you, secure you a burrow, and bare their teeth at your enemies. Is this not what marriage is all about?"

From *Everyman's Guide to the Modern Universe and Household Management*, Nathaniel P. Speck, Professor of Medieval History, St Simons University, Chisholm, Nova Scotia

Eleven

"What we're talking about here is a completely non-repressive society – one in which the natural human drives, the passionate attractions, would be elevated, nurtured and cultivated! A self-contained community where labour would be joyous, where everyone could pursue their natural desires for variety, in work and in love. Where women would no longer be trapped in the drudgery of domestic work, and everyone would be freed up to pursue their interests and desires. To the benefit of all!"

Tabitha was at her most disarming, at the lecture podium. About Fourier, she was passionate and eloquent. She quoted him in the original French, sending her students scurrying to the library after class, pounded down on the podium to make a particular point, revealed the little-known fact that Fourier was the first person to use the word "feminisme." She drew elaborate charts on the overhead, the startling changes in the universe Fourier had mapped out for a period of 70,000 years, as the planets and the stars, guided by their own passionate laws of attraction, drew themselves closer to earth and harmony began to emerge.

The Fourier tree of passions – four affective, three distributive, the butterfly, the composite, their swirling, interdependent lives in the phalanx. She showed them maps of phalanx experiments, the gardens and the conservatories, the interconnected buildings. She quoted from letters and diaries about life on the phalanx at the turn of the nineteenth century. And she was able to announce that she had plans to turn all this textbook stuff into a reality!

"Consider what Emerson had to say about Fourier – he imagined hundreds of phalanxes side by side – what tillage, what architecture, what refectories, what dormitories, what reading rooms, what concerts, what lectures, what gardens, what baths! Just imagine it!"

"Critics denounce him as a fanatic! Well, so be it! If you were a visionary, wouldn't you be? But let's be reasonable. Fourier was light years ahead of his time. His systematic critique of work, marriage, even patriarchy was truly radical! He predated women's liberation! Modern educational theory! Gay rights!"

And into this fist-pounding, heart-racing, passionate celebration of Utopian socialism came Laura MacDonald, housewife, and part-time entrepreneur. She decided to sign up for Tabitha's course in a perverse desire for revenge. She would size her up, shatter her theories on paper, stand up to her in class. She would embarrass her in front of her students, complain about her classroom methods to the Dean. It wasn't because of love. Laura felt she could fling Brian off her like a tattered sock and not experience any regret whatsoever, except that she had wasted so much time with him. But that Laura could have been bored and dissatisfied for so long, and done nothing about it, and that he had been the one to stray, this was too vexing altogether. Something had to be done.

As Tabitha began her attacks on conventional morality, the sworn enemy of Fourier's passionate attractions, Laura's first impulse was to go limp, determined to be bored by this atrocious woman who'd been screwing around with her husband. But, over the weeks, eventually the words began to sink in. Revenge began to be usurped by a more interesting rival – curiosity. And while

157

it was true that Tabitha had stolen one life away from her, she had given her back another, one whose promise was far more enriching than the other. Besides, Tabitha's bombast in class was hard to escape. Maybe he had a point, Laura thought. After all, as Fourier said, morality teaches us to be at war with ourselves. Maybe it was time for something else.

It wasn't easy for Laura to be back at school. Of course everyone thought she had burned Tabitha's house down, since everyone knew about the affair, being such a small town, and while this gave her a certain élan at Sobeys, it made her the object of microscopic attention at St Simons. And she had thought about it, she had to admit. The students stared and whispered when she came into the lecture hall.

The notoriety was pretty good for business, but being the focus of so much fascination made her uncomfortable. She wanted to be outdoors, recording daily rainfall and cloud cover, comparing air temperature to freezing patterns, conducting frog surveys, doing research. It had taken her nearly forty years and the thought of criminal activity to set her straight on who she was and what she wanted to do with her life. But what to do with the life she had already started?

Laura and Brian didn't talk much anymore. The household routines continued, the wash got done and the clothes folded, the meals cooked and the dishes washed, but slowly, ever so slowly, Fourier was beginning to creep into their lives. Laura was forced to admit she was mesmerized by Tabitha's lectures, by the passion she brought to her life, by her audacious plans to establish a phalanx, right there in clannish Chisholm.

Her children consoled themselves with the word that was going around at school – that their mother had just gone through a short fit of being "mental" – even though Michael would ask every so often, usually over his Fruit Loops in the morning: "Mummy isn't going to burn our house down, is she?"

"Don't be silly, Michael," Brian would reply, but without a stirring sense of conviction, and so doubt was introduced into the household, making every transaction perilous and loading conversations with double and triple meanings. Of course Laura was never charged, there was never any proof of how the fire was started at all, no one having discovered the charred remains of a grasshopper burned to a crisp next to a pile of Tabitha's household wiring, and so the doubts grew stronger, unimpeded by the truth, and Brian, although he wanted to, could never bring himself to ask her. The idea that his wife might have set someone's house on fire because of an affair was like a badge of honour for Brian, and this ordinary little man, plumped up by the idea that his wife had flown into a fit of uncontrollable, jealous rage, did not really want to know otherwise. And so they continued, in a wary little sidestepping dance, to pretend they were married, to wave at the neighbours from the icy silence of their car, smiling, and to peck each other's cheeks at various functions. They appeared together before their children and made small talk, filled lunch kits, whipped up macaroni and cheese, and played *Sorry* and *Frustration* in the evenings with the children before they went to bed. They met their teachers and signed off on report cards. They modelled themselves on the other marriages that played out around them, at least until bedtime.

Although Brian had held back for weeks after Laura confronted him about the affair, one night he could no longer stand the grim silence that hung around their bed. Laura had her nose in a book, as she usually did. That night it was *Fourier at Brook Farm – The American Experiment*. She didn't look up as Brian took off his clothes and got into his pyjamas, the very act that had been so insignificant for so many years suddenly huge and uncomfortable, every elastic difficult to manage, his socks stiff and unyielding as he tried to pull them off his feet, his pants lumpy and noisy, a pair of elephant trunks. As he did up the buttons on his pyjamas, he cleared his throat and tried to get Laura's attention, but she was staring into the exotic text of her book and refusing to look up. He crawled into bed beside her, lifting the sheets so that a vague breeze blew across their legs. Laura tugged the covers back up to her chest, and turned the page. Brian stared over at her until she was forced to look his way.

"Something you need?"

Brian raised and lowered his eyebrows several times, in a way that used to make her laugh, but it no longer worked. She turned back to her book.

Brian could see the tops of her breasts at the edge of the cover, their soft white half moons making him crazy with desire. He put his finger under the thin silk strap of her nightgown and let it drop off her shoulder, then leaned over to kiss her. Laura flinched back, as if she had been sprayed with mace.

"Get off me."

Brian flounced back on his pillow, and stared up at the ceiling.

"Jesus Christ Laura, we're married, aren't we?"

Laura didn't answer him.

"Well, this Fourier fellow, isn't he supposed to be a champion of free love and all that? Where's the free love in this family, I'd like to know."

"You don't get it, Brian, you just don't get it. It's not about promiscuity, it's about passion."

Brian lurched in the bed, as if he'd been stung by an electric shock, and slapped himself back against the pillow.

"Oh, right, let's get all technical here. It's about fucking, am I right?"

"Brian, keep your voice down, the children."

Brian mimicked her in a silly falsetto. "Brian, keep your voice down..."

Laura flung the covers off and got out of bed.

"That's it, I'm sleeping downstairs."

"Fine, go ahead."

Brian slumped over in the bed, sending Laura's book tumbling to the floor where a sheaf of notes fell out, research notes for Laura's term paper: "What price liberty? Weighing the exponential scale of love in Harmony." He tried to pull the covers up, but they had slipped half off the bed along with the book. He bunched them up towards his neck, but most of his back was now fully exposed to the chill. He closed his eyes, and tried to pretend he was comfortable.

No Finer Joy than a Woman of Wise and Sound Judgment
    "Riches you may have, fine clothes, good looks, noble birth – but there is no finer joy than to be in the company of a woman of wise and sound judgment. Even if your heart is sick, or grieving, or nailed shut by an endless string of disappointments, a woman of chaste and feminine virtue will lift your spirits and convince you that all is right with the world, and with you. Be careful in conversation, and do not mock her honest and guileless ways – for she believes in you, as no one else does."

    From *Everyman's Guide to the Modern Universe and Household Management*, Nathaniel P. Speck, Professor of Medieval History, St Simons University, Chisholm, Nova Scotia

Twelve

Life with Fiona and Tabitha hadn't turned out quite as badly as Nathaniel had feared. In fact, they had settled into a few reliable patterns that could easily compete for comfort with the best of marriages. Ever since the arrival of Fiona, his clothes, ancient and tattered as they were, were always pressed and reasonably clean. He wore the same time-worn jackets and tweeds, the same Prospector workboots, with their steel-enhanced toes and braided laces, the same faded grey scarf in winter...none of these had changed. Nor had Nathaniel forsworn the truly enormous parka which he donned as the first snow began to fall, padded with goose down and trimmed with real fur, the warmest and most ridiculous looking thing he had ever owned.

It couldn't be said that Nathaniel swaggered, or that his step was even remotely jaunty. He didn't leer at women or imagine himself transformed into a Jean-Pierre. But he no longer raced from class to class, puffing and sweating in the way only a really big man can. He paused, he reflected, he moved with the calm assurance of someone who knows that whatever happens, the world will wait. Students, secretaries, the chair of the department. They will all wait.

And how did he know? Because at home, women waited for him. The knowledge of these women, real women tucked into the rooms of his house, gave Speck a completely new way of seeing the world. Nathaniel's slow and steady ways won back the hearts of some of his students, who now felt perfectly comfortable stopping him in the hallway and asking for extra help with a paper, or some direction for research. "Have a good day," Nathaniel was rumoured to have uttered, to the complete astonishment of his students. A whole new mythology was born, with Nathaniel at the centre. Having opened his doors to not one but two women in need Nathaniel had won the respect of his peers, and more than a little curious tongue wagging. "He's a big man," the administrative assistant to the Dean whispered to the rector's assistant over coffee, "You know what that means." "Big enough for two?" the other replied, and giggled. Nathaniel Speck was fast becoming a legend.

Fiona was an early riser, and was usually up well before Nathaniel, padding around the kitchen in her pink bunny-eared slippers and making tea, adding homey touches like a tea cozy shaped like an English country cottage and a set of hand-painted egg cups that hung on a wooden stand in the corner.

Nathaniel usually staggered out of bed, rumpled and grumpy, at about ten, unless he had an early class. And Tabitha followed soon after, sleepy, but civil. But instead of facing the dim curtained dark of an empty kitchen, Nathaniel now walked into the bright lights of a Fiona morning – tea made, kitchen tidied, and on some mornings, the small and endearing little bald head of a soft-boiled egg was ready for him at the kitchen table, set out in its egg cup and waiting to be cracked open. Fiona was, by and large, a good-natured soul. She had calmed down considerably since that first encounter, but her speech was still filled with expletives, and Nathaniel was actually getting used to it.

"I've been fiddling with this fucking tea kettle all morning Nathaniel and I can't seem to get the twist out of the cord here."

"Here, let me see." And this, oh this is what made life with Fiona and Tabitha such bliss for Nathaniel. If he wanted an intellectual discussion, he could seek out Tabitha. And with Fiona, he could come to her side, and he could fix things. Despite her age Fiona was in some ways like a child, and Nathaniel's big, calm, and expansive voice could evaporate her restless energies, quiet her down. It was almost as if the three of them had come together as a composite soul – echoing Fourier's idea that multitudes were always preferable to the solitary, that is to say, dinner alone was one of the worst crimes of civilization. In turn, Nathaniel's heart began to grow and expand. It wasn't that Nathaniel was falling in love with Fiona, despite his youthful adoration and the rather endearing characteristics she had acquired in middle age, but that around Fiona, he didn't feel as big and blundering, as clumsy, and as ill equipped to deal with the world.

For Fiona, he mended broken teacups (which she had broken during long and bitter phone conversations with Dick), so invisibly you would be hard pressed to see where the thin line of glue was; sewed on buttons because she had lost her glasses and couldn't see to thread the needle; even managed to save poor old Bill from the embarrassment of having his arthritic legs go underneath him by administering small doses of glucosamine sulfate in with his dog chow.

Fiona made no demands on Nathaniel, except to be there, to be in his house. Tabitha made no demands either, simply worked late into the night at her laptop, fleshing out theories of composite attractions and industrial enterprise. Much of the rest of the time she was at her office at the university. Some evenings they sat in the living room, facing out to Bluejacket Bay and watching the sun go down, sipping their tea in highly companionable silence. One night, Fiona asked about the naming of the bay. Tabitha was at the university teaching a late night tutorial.

"It's fucking beautiful, Nathaniel, really it is. But it's sad too, do you know what I mean? There's something sad about that water."

Nathaniel blew across the surface of his tea, creating small shivering ripples.

"It's a sad story."

Fiona turned in her chair, and spread the grey-coloured afghan she had knit from Nathaniel's old wool socks (hoarded, for some purpose, for years) across her knees.

"Tell me."

Nathaniel put his tea down on the floor beside him, and cleared his throat.

"He was an only child, a shy, intelligent boy, whose parents weren't quite right. I think we'd call it Down syndrome now, but back then they said they just weren't right in the head. They lived over there, where that cottage is now, but before it was more like a shack."

As Nathaniel spoke, cars passing on the road below spread their lights over the two of them like a peacock opening its feathers. Their two faces suddenly brightened, and then the room was dim again, and the story continued, each detail lending weight to the detail that went before.

"They tried their best to give Daniel, that was his name I think, a normal life, the best they could. They sent him to school, and they mended his clothes, and everybody around here tried to help them out with food parcels and old clothes. He loved them not only because they were all he had, but because of who they were, and of how hard they worked to make a life for him. But one, bitter winter, the winter Daniel turned twelve, something terrible happened."

Fiona gazed over at Nathaniel, a kind of dumb rapture on her face, for while she wasn't falling in love either, a kind of comfortableness in her bones was settling over her, a fitting in of a sort she wasn't used to. The sound of Nathaniel's deep and melodious voice was knitting someone new from the old threads.

"Daniel was very late coming back from school. The bus had lost a wheel turning on an icy curve and the children were taken into the McGregor's house until it was fixed, the nearest house to the road."

Nathaniel was a born storyteller, with his resonant, romantic voice and his articulate syntax. Fiona was a born listener, snuggled in her woolly cocoon, conjuring up Daniel, his family, even the swerve of the bus as it rounded the corner, the fear on the pale faces of the children. She supposed it was probably the ability to imagine that had kept her marriage afloat for so long, gathering up the good parts like crumbs and making more of them than she should have.

"By the time Daniel made it home it was well past midnight. It was a terrible storm, the ice lashing out like whips and almost no visibility at all, but Daniel's parents, sick with worry, had gone out into the storm to look for him. They had no phone to call anyone. They just followed their instincts and went out into the storm. They lost their bearings, and couldn't find their way back."

Fiona sucked in her breath, and then stifled an involuntary yawn, a strange little gurgling sound coming from the back of her throat. She tried to stop it, and choked a little. Nathaniel pointed to her teacup and carried on while Fiona slurped and tried to relax.

"When Daniel finally found them, so it goes, he thought they had already frozen to death, the two of them, but he took off his blue jacket anyway and placed it over them, as if to warm them. Then he curled up next to them, until the storm passed. They lived, but poor Daniel, he froze to death."

Fiona sat slumped in the chair, tears streaming down her face, trying to wipe them away with what remained of Nathaniel's old socks.

"I'll never be able to look at that water the same way again. Never."

Nathaniel stood up in his chair, and stretched his arms up above his head, and for a moment he towered over Fiona like a giant. She wondered if he was about to sweep her up in his arms. But instead, he simply smiled and looked out across the bay.

"It's only a story, Fiona. I don't know if any of it's true. A boy froze to death there, that I know. The rest, well, it's a theory. "

Nathaniel ruffled Fiona's soft, fine-haired head and laughed, a deep, throaty chuckle.

"You shouldn't let it upset you."

Fiona snuffled and blew her nose, shook her head. She felt curiously betrayed, as if Nathaniel had told her an abject lie, straight to her face, and then laughed at her for believing it.

"Why'd you tell me that story? It's going to fucking haunt me now. "

Just then Bill jumped up on Fiona's lap, newly chipper since taking the glucosamine and positively benevolent towards Nathaniel, who mostly ignored him, even as he followed him from room to room, even as Nathaniel shut the door regularly on his curious, twitching wet nose. It occurred to Nathaniel one day that Bill was slowly turning into Fiona. He'd heard it before, that dogs and their owners began to resemble each other over the years, and from time to time there was a look in Bill's eye that called up Fiona in a way that was positively unnerving.

But Nathaniel hadn't heard the question. He'd already disappeared down the hall and bolted into the safety of his study.

Fiona had simply asked her question into the darkness. And it seemed to her, that as life metaphors went, this one pretty much summed it up.

On Doing Lunch with One's Spouse

"There is nothing so sad as the promise of a lunch with one's beloved that proves to be a minefield of falsehoods. Lunch with a spouse should be reserved for that most precious of encounters — a meal taken outside the home, husband and wife taking a little extra care with their dress and deportment, a little lift in the step. Such a lunch should not be marred by discord or indigestion. Celebrate the endless rediscovery of one's spouse over the midday meal, seen in a new light from across the table, the white linens, of your favourite restaurant."

From *Everyman's Guide to the Modern Universe and Household Management*, Nathaniel P. Speck, Professor of Medieval History, St Simons University, Chisholm, Nova Scotia

Thirteen

Laura arranged to meet Brian at The Lobster Trap, the only moderately fancy restaurant in the area, even though it was out on the highway and as tacky as highway restaurants come. She didn't want to face him at home, or with the children around. The restaurant was decorated with lobster traps inhabited by grinning plastic lobsters, and the traps were arranged on shelves hanging from the ceiling by industrial yet worn-looking chains, so that wherever you sat in the restaurant, you weren't completely sure one wasn't about to fall on your head. Laura had named it The People Trap, referring both to the perilous crustaceans and also to the prices. A few stringy and pitifully small shreds of lobster, doused in a red sauce that was mostly ketchup, was tarted up and sold for $18.95 to unsuspecting tourists as "Lobster Divine." But if you were a local, you could get away with $9.95 for a home-made clam chowder that wasn't half bad and some bread rolls, which, while unassuming, were at least warm. The restaurant was divided into two halves, one was the restaurant proper and the other half was a kind of bar, where you could get snacks.

The restaurant proper tended to be the domain of anyone who came from at least five miles out of town; the bar was mostly populated by the locals. It was divided by an aquarium, where grumpy-looking fish eyed both sides from their tank, which was sticky with the fingerprints of children who liked to rattle the fish by tapping on the sides, despite the sign taped on the front which said "Please Do Not Bother the Fish," a concept not readily understood by children who had grown up near the water and who viewed fish not exactly as creatures with feelings, but mostly as a principal food group.

Laura arrived early, so she could choose an appropriate table, and was shown initially to the worst table in the restaurant by Muriel Reilly, the proprietor's wife, who managed to be both haughty and dowdy at the same time. Muriel didn't approve of Laura and her messing around in other people's bedrooms. And besides, her sister had called in Laura with that ridiculous sheet business, and her husband was so mad when he found out he'd run off to Halifax to take up the guitar and live at the Y. Muriel placed Laura at the drafty table by the door. Laura shook her head and looked around. It was only 11:30. The restaurant was completely empty.

"I'd like another table please."

Muriel didn't say anything, but gestured over by the window. "How's that one?"

"That would be fine. Thank you."

Muriel dumped the menus on the table and turned away.

"Um, excuse me, do you think I could get a glass of dry white wine please?"

"Yup." Muriel disappeared into the kitchen.

Laura looked out of the window at the parking lot, which was empty except for her car and a couple of vans delivering supplies to the restaurant. Beyond that was the highway, the only route out of town, and which led to Halifax.

"Penny for your thoughts."

Brian leaned over to give Laura a perfunctory peck on the cheek, unable to sidestep at least a minimum of convention, but Laura stood back.

"Sit, have some wine."

Laura settled into her chair and Muriel was there in an instant. Brian hadn't betrayed the locals by stepping out on television and making a fool of himself.

"What can I get you, my dear?"

"How are you Muriel? Business good?"

"Can't complain."

"Good, dear, good. Can I have a glass of white please?"

"Coming right up."

If Brian had looked ordinary before, he now looked like the ghost of ordinary. His hair seemed thinner, his face receding into a blank nothingness. Laura no longer ironed his shirts or made him roast beef sandwiches for lunch in the Spider Man lunch kit he had borrowed from his son and taken a liking to, so he had a vaguely rumpled look, and there were faint grease spots on his sleeves.

"Seems odd, coming here. We came here on our first date."

Laura took a large sip of her wine and gazed out the window, remembering that looking through this same window she had always imagined that was the highway that would take them away from Chisholm, its small-town claustrophobia and clannish ways.

"That was a long time ago, Brian."

Brian didn't know what to say. He began flipping the pages of the menu back and forth. He could no longer read his wife. He had no idea what was going on. Sometimes in the small hours of the morning he would wake up and peer into her face while she was still asleep, studying the curves and contours he had known since he was almost a child, and then wonder why she seemed to feel nothing for him, nothing at all. He studied her hands, which knew every inch of him, and wondered if he would ever feel them again, or if she would ever want to. And then he would turn away in the bed, facing the cold wall, and try to sleep.

Laura was glancing down at the Lobster Trap menu too, the catch of the day and lunchtime specials added on a post-it note. She decided to have the battered shrimp, just for the pure joke of it. She closed the menu abruptly, releasing a decisive puff of air, and faced her husband.

"I'm thinking of going back into research. I've started to read up on the latest work."

Brian sighed with relief. He thought she had been about to say she was going to leave him. He raised his glass for a toast.

"To the frogs then!"

Just as their glasses made a joyless clink, Muriel appeared with her order pad.

"Bit of a celebration, is it?"

Laura looked up and frowned.

"We'll both have the battered shrimp, please."

Muriel shuffled off. The restaurant was beginning to fill up – a few tourists driving into town for the Celtic winter games, others on their way to the Cape, one or two neighbours. The town was so small, almost everyone was either a neighbour or a relative. That was something Laura had always hated about Chisholm, one of the things she had wanted to get away from. Until now, she hadn't known how to escape from who she had always been, reading in the faces of everyone she knew a certain way of being, what was expected.

"Will I have to call you Doctor MacDonald from now on?"

Brian was feeling positively jaunty, thinking his wife had forgiven him the affair and was opening a new chapter in their lives. He failed to notice that Laura had bitten her nails down to the quick and had not smiled once since arriving at the restaurant. At that moment, Laura would have been far more comfortable talking about the North American wood frog, how the frog can grind its heartbeat to a complete stop for weeks during hibernation, only to spontaneously recover in the spring.

All things went in cycles, she believed. She thought about the frogs, freezing and thawing, freezing and thawing their way through their short green lives for about the last 190 million years. Just then the battered shrimp arrived.

"What about Twisted?"

Laura began pulling off batter with her fork, revealing a small, pale pink and vaguely translucent shrimp beneath.

"Since when did you care about that?" Laura saw Brian's face and softened. "There's no reason I can't do both. Now that Twisted's a mail-order franchise, it practically runs itself."

Brian was prying the breaded skin from his shrimps and feeling vaguely festive. But Laura poked her fork into his shrimp and stopped him, leaned over to look into his face.

"It was never about the business though, Brian. I wanted to believe that everything was right there, destiny and all, in the sheets, so we'd all know what to do. I wanted a theory that would explain to me why I always felt so empty and disappointed all the time. "

Brian looked confused. The light outside was already beginning to fade, the dark and broody clouds of winter closing in. Cars raced by on the highway, fleeing Chisholm for the lights of Halifax or speeding up now that home was in sight.

"And now I know what I need to do. I'm going to leave you."

The clatter of Brian's fork on the cement floor sent Muriel scurrying towards their table.

"I'll be applying for joint custody of the boys."

Laura threw three twenties on the table and walked out, leaving both Brian and Muriel open mouthed, a state which lasted even as the sun was swallowed up by the gaping maw of night.

Television as the Perpetrator of Human Decline

"*There is a new form of sloth that will surely spell out our decline as a species unless we act on it immediately, and that is television. With its bland expressionless heart facing most of us day and night, we are unable to separate our most private thoughts and desires from those of the television, and this is folly, dear readers, sheer folly. Each night you must cover it with a sack! Rip out the cord from the offending socket! Seal up the remote with glue! But don't dump it into the bay, or leave it out with the trash. Keep it around to remind yourself of how close you have come to self-destruction, and how clever you are to have willed yourself into a different future than that forecast by contemporary culture.*"

From *Everyman's Guide to the Modern Universe and Household Management*, Nathaniel P. Speck, Professor of Medieval History, St Simons University, Chisholm, Nova Scotia

Fourteen

It was a morning of exceptional gloom, and Fiona could find nothing in her domestic routine to save her from its downward spiral into complete and utter depression. She could feel the coming storm right down to the marrow of her bones, which ached in a kind of painful divination. The clouds hung down like faded old jeans, blue-grey, mottled, too heavy even for the sky, and it was so dark Fiona had to turn on lights to see what she was doing. For a few moments they lit up the gloom and made the quiet of the Speck household bearable, but it didn't last long. Fiona poured herself a cup of tea and decided to make a phone call. She had lain awake most nights for weeks thinking about it, after seeing the program on TV, but wondered if she had the nerve to make the call. She set down her teacup, and dialled.

"Twisted Incorporated. Can I help you?"

Fiona cleared her throat.

"Yes, yes. My name is Fiona Barrett, and I saw your show on the cable station?"

"Yes."

"Well, I need you to come over right now and analyze two beds. It's very important."

"We usually make appointments, Miss...what did you say your name was?"

"Barrett, Fiona Barrett. Look, I know I should have an appointment, but it's hard for me to say when people will be here and when they won't, and this morning would be the prefect time, and I haven't touched the beds, and this is like the fucking rest of my life here..."

Fiona's voice got louder and louder, until finally Laura interrupted her.

"I actually have a cancellation today, you're in luck. Give me your address."

"1787 West Bend Road, just across from Bluejacket Bay. The big house at the top of the hill."

"I know it. I'll be around at eleven."

Fiona replaced the receiver. She'd actually done it. She started a little fit of whistling and then stopped herself. After all, it might be bad news. But one way or the other she had to know. I mean, here was Tabitha now, flitting around in her little Chinese slippers and her red silk kimono, sputtering from Fourier in French, a language Fiona abhorred and didn't understand anyway, and the two of them chuckling away at their private jokes. It wasn't that she didn't like Tabitha, in fact she liked her rather a lot, but she needed to know. And so let's get Twisted over, she reasoned, and settle it once and for all.

Laura arrived on the dot at eleven, carrying her small black briefcase and a pocketful of business cards. Fiona didn't think that Laura looked quite as glamorous off the television screen, but she had a pleasant, earnest face, and a professional manner that set Fiona immediately at ease. She offered her coffee, and they sat in the living room, staring out at the bay, the sky a dark violet stain above the wrinkled grey sheen of the water.

"Now, I'll need you to sign a couple of papers for me. The service is entirely confidential, as I guess you know from watching the television program, but I need a little bit of information before I begin."

"Okay, fire away!"

Laura smiled. Fiona wasn't her typical client. In the first place, her sense of urgency seemed to have been replaced with a curious mischief, as if she was fooling a teacher or playing a practical joke. And she hadn't checked off the box for husband, so Laura wondered whose bed it was she wanted analyzed. Most of her clients wanted the lowdown on their spouses, but Fiona seemed a different case entirely.

"Now, you understand that my findings may not always be conclusive. As with any new science, any theory, there are flaws and cases which are not black and white."

"Oh, I understand. I just want some idea. Help me fucking sleep at night."

Laura raised her eyebrows.

"Then let's get started, shall we?"

Laura followed Fiona into a dark bedroom at the end of a long corridor. A single bed was pushed against the wall, and someone had slung an old afghan on top of it, in a kind of concession to order, because everything else seemed in relative disarray. There was an odd smell in the room, a mixture of breath mints and something musky, and there were books everywhere, piled in towers and creating stepladders that rose to nothing. The drawers were open and socks and sweaters were tumbling out, in fact one sock seemed to have defied the force of gravity and appeared to hang in mid-air, held to the drawer by a single thread caught on a splinter in the wood. Against the wall was a four-drawer file cabinet, stuffed with papers that bulged out from the sides. Fiona had long given up clearing up Nathaniel's room for him. As fast as she did it the clutter would creep back and eventually her frustration wore her down. Laura pulled back the afghan decisively, releasing a shot of something vaguely skunky into the room.

The entire top sheet appeared to be held to the bed at one corner, where it bunched together like an accordion. The whole sheet was off centre, three quarters of it falling to the floor, as if someone had been unable to get it straight in the night and simply given up. The pillow was mashed into the wall, and there appeared to be a permanent depression in it the shape of someone's head. The sheets were a pale pink colour, a fact Laura found curious, until Fiona explained that she'd mixed up the sheet sets last laundry day and put the wrong ones on this bed.

"Well, it's obviously a man's bed."

Fiona nodded.

"A man of considerable intellectual prowess."

Fiona was still nodding, like one of those bobble-headed dogs people put in the back windows of their cars.

"A man who craves a woman's touch."

Fiona felt her heart lightening. She knew it, she knew!

"But there are a few problems here."

Fiona's face darkened.

"He has trouble expressing himself out loud. And he may be out of touch with reality. It could be a serious problem."

Fiona thought about Nathaniel's book, which she had finally decided to read after all this time.

"I deduce that he's also a bit of a slob, isn't he?" Laura laughed at her own little joke, but Fiona wasn't smiling. Laura wiped the grin from her face and got ready to survey the next bed. Fiona gestured her out of the room and into Fiona's bedroom at the other side of the house.

When Fiona had arrived, the room was little more than a storage closet, filled to the rims with boxes of household supplies. In the time that she had been there, Fiona had put most of those supplies to use, and so gradually the room had emptied and Fiona had filled it up with her own things. Fiona loved purple, and so the curtains, the bedspread, the cozy throw pillows, and the little round carpet were all in different shades of lavender. Every spare surface seemed festooned with frills, doilies sat under dancing ballerina figurines, and a family of teddy bears, their gauze tummies stuffed with real lavender, were placed on the bed with some care, each one smaller than its neighbour. Laura stepped in and pulled back the purple cover, spilling the bears to the floor.

"Oh, I'm sorry Fiona, I just need to get the cover off as quickly as possible. Makes for a better specimen."

Fiona felt a little uncomfortable thinking of her bed as a specimen, but she smiled at Laura and picked up the bears, waiting for her revelations.

Fiona's sheets were not tucked in anywhere, and Laura had to admit this was the first time she'd encountered such a phenomenon. The sheets lay as if they'd simply floated down there from the sky, one on top of the other, and not a corner, not an edge folded under anywhere. Laura looked puzzled and started rapping her pen on her notebook, as if this would help her figure it out. Fiona looked over, expectantly.

"Fiona, I have to ask, is this your room?"

Fiona, fearing the worst, said yes, but in a voice so soft Laura barely heard her.

"This is your room."

Fiona nodded and gulped.

"I have to say it's the first time I've come across this. You must realize that my analysis may be a little out of whack. I'm entering virgin territory here."

Fiona blushed.

"Well, to start with, I'd suggest a complete lack of guile, something I must say in my business I find highly refreshing."

Laura patted the sheets and sat down on the edge of the bed. Then she noticed the pillow case was simply lying on top of the pillow.

"Remarkable, truly remarkable. As calming as a tide pool you are Fiona, it's all here."

Fiona smiled distractedly, and then bustled over to sit next to Laura. She struggled to find the right words.

"But what I need to know, what I must understand, well, how can I..."

Laura interrupted her.

"You want to know the compatibility factor between this person here," and she pointed with one finger, "and that person across the other side." Laura pulled a massive calculator out of her briefcase and began punching in numbers she'd jotted down in her notebook as she'd gone from room to room. Finally she finished, and was just about to reveal the magic number to Fiona, when Tabitha entered the room.

"Oh, here you are, I was wondering ..." Tabitha suddenly caught sight of Laura, who up to that time had had her head bent forward over her notes. They stared at each other, saying nothing. Fiona's heart was thumping like mad, as she waited for the information that would change her life. But the air was charged with some new tension, and so she held back and said nothing. She tried to crane her neck over to see the number revealed in the big screen of Laura's calculator, but Laura had half hidden it with her hand.

Tabitha still didn't know if Laura knew about the affair or not. Their conversations at school had been civil, but kept to the minimum.

"Laura, it's been a while since you've been to class. I saw you on TV though."

"Yeah, the queen of cable. Big fish in a small pond, I guess."

In class, Tabitha found it hard not to imagine the pallid sex that must have taken place between Brian and Laura. She wondered how Laura could stand it, year after year, and decided that's probably why she had turned to free enterprise as a way of releasing some energy. But here, larger than life and out of context in Fiona's bedroom, with her notebooks and her glasses, it suddenly occurred to Tabitha that Laura was a woman of multiple passions, and that she'd simply failed to see it. La Composite!

"Laura, I know it's early in the day, but it's so gloomy out there I think I'm going to crack open a bottle of sherry and have a glass. What do you say? You too Fiona, how's about a little mid-afternoon tipple?"

Fiona turned to Laura.

"I'm game. How about you?"

Laura hesitated at first, but then considered what awaited her at home. The kids were at her sisters. She felt like a free woman.

"Why not."

"But first, Tabitha, we have a little business to finish up."

Tabitha took her cue and stepped backwards out of the room, bowing all the while. "Meet you in the parlour!" Living with Fiona and Nathaniel had cheered up the gloom she felt after her botched seduction, and concentration on the task at hand, designing the working phalanx, kept her busy enough to avoid a lot of soul-searching. Fourier and his ideas filtered through the house like pure sunlight, warming up the isolation they had all felt for most of their lives. Sketches for buildings and orchards and gardens were taped on the walls from floor to ceiling, making the whole idea seem real, workable, liveable, as if the phalanx itself was growing within the house.

Laura took off her glasses and replaced them in their case. She put her briefcase on the floor, stood up, and straightened up the cover.

"It doesn't look good, Fiona, I'm afraid."

"But, how can you be so sure, I mean, as you said, my case is very unusual. You might be wrong."

"I might very well be wrong, Fiona, and I have been, believe me. And remember, it's only a theory. But when you look at the numbers, it seems fairly clear. My guess is friendship, yes, but anything else..."

All this for a fucking guess, Fiona thought to herself. She could find nothing to say at first, but then she summoned up some of the pluck that had allowed her to escape the clutches of her marriage and piped up in a fatalistic kind of voice.

"Well, friendship is a rare thing, isn't it? Especially in this day and age. And friendship can lead to other things, right?" Fiona picked up one of the lavender bears and held its tummy to her nose, breathing in the smell of the Norfolk fields where the flowers had been grown. She closed her eyes for a moment, conjuring up the great sprawl of lavender spreading for miles throughout the countryside. "Let's go get that drink then, shall we? And what do I owe you?"

The two women found Tabitha already set up in the living room, cut glass sherry glasses filled with amber liquid, a fire in the grate. Laura found it a little unusual, to be sitting here with a dotty hausfrau and her husband's ex-mistress, sharing a drink in the middle of the day, but for some reason it felt more comfortable, more natural than anything she had done for some time. She thought back to what Fiona had said about friendship. Perhaps that's what had been missing all along with Brian. They were Husband and Wife, but they weren't even close to being chums.

Tabitha and Fiona often shared a drink in the afternoon, Fiona having found herself surprisingly grateful for Tabitha's company, especially on the days when Nathaniel locked himself in his study and emerged only to go to the bathroom or to accept a plate of sandwiches.

And once she had opened up, Tabitha had listened with rapt attention to the story of Dick and Fiona many times over, because once it actually came out, it seemed that Fiona never tired of telling it. It had become Fiona's personal mythology, and although the details changed and shifted somewhat with each telling, Fiona began to emerge less and less as the downtrodden victim of Dick's second childhood, and more and more as the heroine. Dick, for all his outwardly appearance of free love, was no more a Fourierite than the Queen of England. But Fiona! Now there was a woman of a different order. She had taken herself and escaped the ridiculous and monogamous limitations of marriage! She was a woman worthy of the phalanx!

And so, during Tabitha and Fiona's afternoon conversations, riddled with sherry, Tabitha had begun the steady conversion of Fiona Barrett to the Utopian ideals of Charles Fourier. She had been unwittingly winning Laura over in class, and Nathaniel, in his typically academic way, had gone out shortly after that first conversation and read everything Fourier had ever written, in its original French.

Tabitha, Fiona and Laura had gone on to their third bottle of sherry when Nathaniel arrived home. Laura was busy telling stories about researching frogs and the three of them were screeching with laughter.

"So like I'm out there, right, and it's pitch dark, and like I'm up to my knees in mud and partly submerged frogs, and I turn on my flashlight! Eureka! Hundreds of eyes, hundreds of froggie eyes all staring at me! It was freaky!"

Tabitha hadn't had this much fun for ages, and even Fiona had to admit they got on well together. Nathaniel walked in, his great burly figure encased in his giant parka making him look bigger than ever, and saw not two but three women curled up around his hearth.

"Time to order a pizza, girls?"

Tabitha got up, awkwardly, and tried not to spill her drink.

"Nathaniel, I don't think you've met Laura. Laura, this is Professor Nathaniel Speck, or, Mister Medieval, as he's best known!"

Laura tried to get up, but couldn't quite make it.

"Just stay there, it's perfectly okay. Nice to meet you. How about a large Hawaiian?"

This brought another fit of giggles from the three women, so Nathaniel decided to just go ahead and order. He pulled four plates down from the shelf and began to set the large rectangular table in the dining room, he even got out napkin rings. There was something festive and portentous in the air, and he wanted to keep it going as long as possible. As he was laying out cutlery and thinking of an appropriate wine to go with pizza, Tabitha put her head around the door.

"Nathaniel, I know we're a little crowded here, but I don't think Laura is in any state to drive. Would you mind if she stayed the night? She'd be fine on the couch."

"It's fine with me, Tabitha, perfectly fine."

"You're a dear. Thanks."

Nathaniel watched Tabitha turn on her heels and head back down the corridor. The lightness of her step made him weak in the knees, it always did, the way women moved like sine waves, all undulating and seamless. He recovered himself, and went to the cellar for a bottle of wine. The sweet sound of women's laughter followed him down the stairs.

Avoiding Frostbite
   "Do not venture blind into the storm. Trouble awaits!"

   From *Everyman's Guide to the Modern Universe and Household Management*, Nathaniel P. Speck, Professor of Medieval History, St Simons University, Chisholm, Nova Scotia

Fifteen

The storm began the very next day, early in the afternoon, at first just a few flakes of snow teasing at the windows and doors. The temperature was moderate, and the children were enjoying it, twirling in figure-eights on their driveways and trying to catch the giant flakes on their tongues. Chisholm began to look like a Christmas card, the snow falling steadily, everything veiled in white polka dots, a painting seen through dotted Swiss. Tabitha looked out of her window at the rest of the university. She had four more papers to mark, and on average each paper took at least forty minutes. Her head ached from all the sherry she'd had to drink the night before. She tried to calculate just how much snow would fall, wondering whether she should leave now and take them with her or finish up here and head home paper-free. Just a little snow, she decided, and plugged in her electric tea maker for a cup of Tetleys, settled down for a few more pathetic interpretations of modern-day Utopia.

Tabitha didn't have a radio or a portable television in her office, so she failed to hear the storm warnings, or the predictions of the worst weather conditions in Maritime history headed for Chisholm that very night. Her office door was shut, and the "Do Not Disturb" sign was hanging on the knob. Jean-Pierre stopped outside at one point, saw the light from beneath the door, and wondered whether to knock and tell Tabitha about the storm, but he saw the sign and reconsidered. There was a rather long list tacked to Tabitha's door – reasons to warrant interruption. Jean-Pierre did not see impending storm on the list, although imminent doom was there. He decided to respect the list and walked on, and Tabitha continued with her papers, as the snow began blowing into heaps and the wind picked up, the temperature falling and the snow easing up to make room for a chill so intense you could get frostbite without gloves. At one point Tabitha looked up from her desk and realized that the view from her window was completely obliterated by the snow. She glanced at her watch. It was only 4:30, but the sky she could only just make out through cracks in the snow looked dark and foreboding. She decided she should probably stay put, keep on marking until things cleared up. She'd done it before, slept curled on the leather armchair that was now piled with papers. But just as she was about to make herself cozy, the phone rang. She saw it was Nathaniel's number flashing.

"Professor Black here."

"Tabitha, thank goodness I reached you. It's Fiona. I don't like the look of this storm. I think you should head on home right away."

Tabitha remembered Nathaniel telling her that Fiona hated storms. Maybe she was just nervous.

"Where's Nathaniel?"

"I'm not sure, working in the study I think, but you know it's pretty bad. They're calling it the worst storm in Maritime fucking history."

Tabitha peered out her window, although she could barely see anything.

"I can see it's bad, but I think I'll stay put and ride it out here. Driving's probably treacherous."

Fiona's voice had risen to a near hysteria, faced with Tabitha's calm resolve.

"But you can't! What if there's a fucking power outage? What if there's no fucking heat? You could fucking freeze to death." Tabitha could gauge Fiona's level of distress by the rising number of expletives. "We've got the wood stove here, the fireplace, the generator. What if this goes on for days and you're fucking trapped there?"

"Okay, okay, I guess you're right. If there's going to be a catastrophe, I might as well be at home!"

"Oh, thank God. I'll put on the tea. See you soon, Tabitha."

Tabitha replaced the receiver and gathered up her papers, unplugged the tea maker, turned out the lights and stepped into the hallway. There was something comforting about having someone worrying about you, and it was a feeling that Tabitha wasn't at all accustomed to. She wondered if she should stop somewhere on the way and buy Fiona some flowers.

As she entered the hallway there was no sound. Everyone else had left. She pressed the button on the elevator and descended through the tower.

The blowing snow was so thick she could barely see her way to the car, but she had done the trip so many times she knew her way by instinct. She managed to get the key in the lock, but the key wouldn't turn. She fumbled in her purse for the lock de-icer which Jean-Pierre, in one of his more helpful moments, had told her she should always have with her in winter in Chisholm. She squirted it on the key and forced some into the lock. Her hands were red and painful from the cold. Finally the key turned in the lock and she tumbled inside, slammed the door shut, and turned the engine on.

As Tabitha was making her slow way home in the storm, Fiona was standing at Nathaniel's back door shouting for Bill to come in. For some reason, Bill had been scratching and pawing and rattling at the back door so pointedly that Fiona had decided to simply open it and show him what lay in store out there. But in a wholly unexpected fit of canine logic Bill had not cowered in the doorway and headed back inside for the easy chair but shot out the door and into the storm. Fiona could barely keep the door open, and her shouts got blown away by the wind, but she stood there shouting anyway, unable to see a thing but the blinding snow and the darkness. Nathaniel was in his study working, and Fiona had strict instructions from him not to disturb him when the study door was closed. This instruction she took seriously, and so instead of going to Nathaniel for help, she threw on Nathaniel's giant blue parka and headed out into the night to look for Bill. Bill's leash lay unaccounted for by the back door, the only clue as to what had happened when Nathaniel emerged from his study to get a cup of tea, and found both Bill, and Fiona, missing.

Nathaniel had been holed up in his study working on the sequel to his book. The idea for a sequel had come to him in a torment one Saturday afternoon, as he was formulating an appropriate translation for a medieval text on housekeeping, fourteenth-century style. Tabitha was hanging laundry on a rack Nathaniel had rigged up in the laundry room, Fiona was cooking beets in the kitchen, and it had suddenly occurred to Nathaniel that volume two of the contemporary home companion was just what the world needed.

If Fiona had had such a companion, perhaps she wouldn't have ended up with a man like Dick, Nathaniel reasoned. If Tabitha had had such a companion, perhaps she wouldn't have ended up sleeping with just about every man on and off campus. Except him, Nathaniel was forced to add. It was to be another masterful tome based on compassion and mutual respect, a guide that would be at once practical, scholarly, and spiritual – comprehensive, accessible, and helpful. He planned to base the organization and format on the fourteenth-century text he had already translated. It was a fabulous idea, brilliant!

Trying to find modern parallels for the subjects listed in the medieval home companion kept Nathaniel preoccupied and awake at nights. A dish for unexpected guests didn't tax the mind too much, but what to do with sections like "Take Your Chickens and Cut Their Throats," or "Sloth and Idleness Beget Evil?" And so although he had currently completely failed to observe one of the worst storms ever whirling about his house like a tornado, Nathaniel had become a keen observer of every detail of his own household, soaking up the day-to-day routines to translate into his book of good counsel. Needless to say, Nathaniel didn't actually participate much in any of it, so his advice was somewhat of a theoretical nature, but this was a stance that, as an academic, Nathaniel was entirely comfortable with.

Nathaniel had watched closely as Tabitha ground coffee beans, in spurts, so as to properly distribute the oil, peered attentively as Fiona filled the cavity of a chicken with lemon and garlic. He took note of the smells of laundry in from the outdoor line, and marvelled at the swing of the axe as Tabitha split logs for the fireplace, a newly developed skill she had acquired as winter fast approached. He watched the women of his household, their twists and turns, their wonderfully indefinable presence, and sometimes, when the two women went together for walks in the woods surrounding his house, Nathaniel would lie down in their beds, smelling the sweetness of the differences between them – a light smell like rain and lavender on Fiona's pillow, Tabitha's musky and dark-blooming, like an orchid at night.

But tonight, as Nathaniel opened the back door to the storm, he knew that something had gone horribly wrong. As he opened the door, a meat packer's billow of cold steamy air rushed in and then simply hung there. Nathaniel's eyes stung from the frigid cold, and he couldn't see anything except a commotion of snow and wind and if you poked through it, the dark night out there, blinded itself by the storm. He knew that Fiona was out there somewhere, lost, looking for Bill, and he knew he had to go out there and find her. He reached for his parka, which was gone, and then for the next nearest warm item of clothing, a fleece of some sort he had picked up somewhere, and he bolted out the door, calling Fiona's name. Miraculously, just as Nathaniel stepped outside, Bill appeared out of the haze of storm and bluster, like a ghost dog emerging through a time warp, and shot up the back stairs and past Nathaniel into the warmth of the house. Nathaniel cursed, and slammed the door behind him.

Tabitha had almost made it round the worst bend of the road leading up to the long driveway into Nathaniel's house, when her car veered off the road and into the ditch. It happened almost lazily, the car just went off in a kind of queasy spin, and suddenly there she was, in the snow bank, adrift, but alive, thank God. For a strange and silly moment Tabitha wondered if she had damaged her car, but then she remembered the storm, and the cold, and everything she had ever learned about hypothermia. She fiddled with the dial on the radio, which was, surprisingly, still working.

"A bone-chilling mass of arctic air has settled over the Chisholm region, snarling traffic and closing all bridges due to the extremely icy conditions. The temperature — a frost-biting minus 29 degrees, and falling."

She switched it off. She shouldn't have stopped off for the flowers at Sobeys. She looked over at them, six wilting pink roses, their edges curled brown. Tabitha tried ramming the gear stick into low, trying to force her way out of the snow bank. The tires spun and moaned underneath her, but it was clear, that for all the effort, nothing was going to budge. One of her headlights was still working, and it lit up the frenzied patterns of the snow ahead, and the darkness behind it. Tabitha tried to force the driver's door open, but somehow it had jammed and wouldn't open. Then she tried the window. As the first blast of cold hit, her eyes immediately filled up with tears, the chill slapping her in the face. Her breath came out in icy clouds, as she struggled to push herself through the window. It occurred to her, in a deranged moment, that she should not have consumed those two apple fritters at lunch. Goddamn Tim Hortons. She remained stuck halfway through, until one major shove jolted her out of the window and into the snow.

Then she remembered her emergency kit, packed away in the glove compartment. She had put it together with Jean-Pierre's help, back then when they had been an item. A bright silver emergency blanket, some chocolate, waterproof matches, candles, and a flare. She had put it all in an old cosmetic bag, a freebie she had received with the purchase of some expensive face cream. She laughed when she thought of the bag, and it had been a bit of a joke between them, because the promotion had been in the summer, and the bag was shaped like a giant beach umbrella, done in the pinks and pastel colours of summer. Along the bottom was a see-through pocket filled with real sand, which swirled back and forth when you tipped the bag. The idea of it being stuffed with emergency supplies needed only in the worst of winter was just the kind of ironic joke that Tabitha loved, except of course that she'd never expected to have to use it.

She contorted herself back in the car and pulled it from the glove compartment. She took off her gloves to try her cellphone, but she remembered that the batteries were dead. She had intended to recharge it that night. Her fingers immediately went numb and she stuffed them as quickly as she could back inside the gloves, cursing their ridiculous fashionability as she attempted to separate each finger into the right hole. She tucked the emergency bag inside her coat, and began the climb up the hill towards Nathaniel's house, the exertion for a while warming her up, as she began to feel the sweat trickle down her chest. She focused all her energies on climbing the hill, making it to the top, finding refuge for a second time in Nathaniel's house. After all the walks she had taken around the property, she imagined she would have had a better sense of direction, but all she could do was head blindly up, her legs dragging in the deepening snow. It had occurred to her to set off the flare and wait by the car for help, but she doubted anyone was even out that night to see it, so she decided against it. Nathaniel's house, Nathaniel's house, she found herself chanting in time with her steps, pushing aside the low-lying branches and their snow weight, feeling the lumps fall and cascade down her neck.

It had been about twenty minutes, but it felt like hours. By now Tabitha's clothing was wet from perspiration and snow and it stuck, like a wet, cold, clammy hand across her back. Her muscles began to ache and then the shivering started. She was almost at the top of the hill, and for a while she stopped, looked around, tried to get her bearings. She fumbled under her coat for the emergency bag, and then realized with a shudder of horror that it wasn't there anymore. She must have dropped it! She tried to retrace her steps in the snow, but they were already covered over. She fumbled around in the snow with her gloved fingers, by now feeling confused even about whether she was standing up or bending over, but found nothing. Maybe she should have stayed near the car, at least there was some protection from the wind and the cold. She fumbled some more and then, miracle of miracles, found it. She held it up and laughed, a kind of crazed and melancholy laugh, as she tilted it this way and that, the sand racing back and forth in its little see-through prison.

Tabitha noticed that her muscles had seized up and she walked with a stiff gait towards what she thought was the crest of the hillside. She couldn't seem to relax them, both legs felt heavy as lead. She had to stop, she had to rest. Under the silvery blanket, she imagined, her thoughts clouded over and she staggered towards the dim shadow of what appeared to be a tree.

Tabitha huddled in the snow beside the tree, and tried to make herself an insulating cover of snow. By now, exhausted, Tabitha looked down at her watch, lit up with the wonder of Indiglo. But the numbers didn't make any sense, they just spun around like a compass dial in Tabitha's head. Why was she even looking at her watch, she asked herself, but couldn't quite answer.

Dropping down in the soft, inviting snow she was grateful for a moment just to stop. Suddenly she saw a figure approaching in the distance. A bear! Tabitha shrieked, or at least thought about it, but was too tired to utter a sound. The hulking figure, shaggy and matted with snow, lurched towards her, and despite her groggy, half-frozen state she realized there was something vaguely familiar about the sight. It was the way he moved, the hulking force of his gait as he stumbled towards her. She didn't know if minutes passed or hours. She drifted off, thinking about life on the phalanx, the idyllic patterns spreading before her like a calm, clear sky. On any given day, the pleasure of five meals, a concert, an hour or two at the library. In the morning, fishing, hunting, or tending to the gardens, in the afternoon, time would be divided among the fish ponds, the sheep pasture or the green-houses. Her eyes fluttered and closed. She was so tired.

Nathaniel finally reached her and gasped when he saw who it was. He leaned over and put his head close to her chest. He pulled the fleece open a little and felt the cool marble of her skin, and listened. At first there was nothing, but then, almost inaudibly, a beat, faint, irregular, but there all the same. He fell back, relieved. He could almost go to sleep, he too was so tired, he had been searching the woods for what seemed like hours, but he grabbed for the little bag that Tabitha had dropped beside her. Beside it, six pale pink blooms lay partly buried in the snow. His fingers fumbled with the bag, they were so cold, he could hardly get the zipper undone, the cold metal seemed to sear through his gloves to the bones of his fingers. He tried to light the matches, but every time one took, the wind snuffed it out. But it doesn't matter, he thought, senselessly, I am getting warmer anyway, in fact, I think I've developed a fever. He longed to just peel off his jacket, his sweater, anything to feel cool again. But he was still level-headed enough to know that their best bet was the emergency blanket. He fumbled with it and drew it out, then he remembered something he had read about hypothermia, or was it something in a James Bond movie? His mind was rambling now, racing and rambling and clouding over with confusion. He was looking for Fiona, but he was so cold now and so disoriented, he doubted he could be any help, wherever she was. But here was someone he could save.

Skin to skin, that's the best way to stay warm, he recalled. He undid the buttons of Tabitha's shirt, climbed on top of her, then awkwardly wrapped the two of them in the silver foil thermal blanket. His skin felt as if it was on fire, he could no longer tell if the thumping he experienced was his own heart or Tabitha's. Tabitha opened her eyes for a second, but seemed to see nothing, and then closed them again. "There, there," Nathaniel said, "there, there." Then she fell out of consciousness, her head resting beside Nathaniel's, the soft, silent snow quilting a cocoon all around them, the silver of the thermal blanket glistening in the cold clear light of the moon.

Fiona had long ago given up on finding Bill, and to her surprise, had retraced her steps easily back to the house. Bill was there to greet her, but she realized in a moment of pure terror that Nathaniel was not. As she hung up the great blue parka she noticed that Nathaniel's old fleece was gone, and so were his Prospector boots. It was with a sickening lurch of heart that Fiona realized Nathaniel must have gone out into the storm looking for her. She had to do something. She had to take action, and quickly.

Fiona ran into the living room, where Laura had passed out on the couch the night before, and was still lying there. Bill was grovelling beside his empty food dish, completely unaware of the effect he had triggered in his doggy pursuit of innocent adventure. She shook Laura awake.

"What? Where am I? Who are you?"

Fiona shook Laura again and then bumped her squarely on the side of the head.

"Don't go all stupid on me, I'm in a bit of a fucking fix here. Nathaniel has gone missing in the storm. I'm all alone here and he's probably been out there for hours and..."

Laura cut her off mid-sentence. She could hear the panic in Fiona's voice as it rose and the words sputtered out faster and faster. She sat up, and her head ached.

"Calm down Fiona. What storm? Tell me exactly what happened."

Laura had always been good in emergencies. In fact, better at emergencies than normal life. Maybe it had had something to do with the amount of time she had spent in the woods doing research, always prepared for any medical emergency, always equipped. She knew that the most important survival tactic was to simply stay calm.

Laura listened as Fiona explained the sequence of events.

"Look, Tabitha's out in the storm somewhere too. I've been trying to reach her on her cell. She was down at the university, but I imagine she's left by now. I'll try her again. They could both freeze to death out there. He's probably a frozen fucking block of ice! Oh my God."

Fiona began crying and Laura chose the wrong moment to throw in one of her favourite old lines about hypothermia.

"Fiona – you ain't dead till you're warm and dead."

The shock of this response allowed Fiona to recover what was left of her self-composure but did not supply the gumption for her to ask Laura what the fuck she meant by that and so she simply stood holding the phone and staring out the window, tears streaming down her cheeks, while Bill rolled over and lay begging at her feet.

It was handy that Fiona had a cryobiologist on her couch to help her out.

"Listen, we'll get through this together. It's really easy to kill somebody if you don't know what you're doing."

By now Fiona was somewhat on the mend. "That's fucking reassuring."

Laura went out to her car and opened the trunk and took out her large yellow flashlight, an axe, and an emergency medical kit.

"Do you have any idea which way he went?"

Laura stood and flashed the light around the property. She imagined she could see the yellow eyes of deer and other creatures staring back at her from the woods, their eyes lit up like stars, but there was nothing there but darkness and trees. For a moment she remembered those frogs, that night.

Fiona pointed towards the woodshed, a favourite hideout of Bills.

"I'm not sure, but probably that way. You see, it's all my fault, he was looking for me, and I was looking for Bill, and…"

"It's okay, everything will be okay. You just go and put the kettle on for some hot tea. I'm sure they'll want some when I find them." Laura considered how ludicrous this must have sounded, given the gravity of the situation, but it seemed to comfort Fiona.

Laura headed for the woods, pulled the soft fur fringe of her hood around her face, and brushed aside the heavy branches with her mitts. She had only gone a few hundred feet when she saw a large hillock glinting in the arc of her flashlight. She looked more closely and realized it wasn't a hillock at all, but what appeared to be two people, not moving, huddled under a blanket of snow. She feared the worst. Opening up the cover on her cell phone she pressed re-dial.

"Fiona. I think I've found him. Actually, I think I've found them both."

Laura moved closer, and saw that it was indeed Nathaniel, nestled peacefully on top of Tabitha.

"Good God. Nathaniel and Tabitha. They look stiff as frozen laundry." Laura addressed this comment to the howling wind. She pulled off her mitt, put out her hand and touched the side of Tabitha's cheek. It felt cold and waxy.

"Are they breathing?" Fiona whispered into the phone.

Laura bent as close as she could, peeling back the stiffened layer of thermal blanket, and listened at Nathaniel's chest.

"I think so. It's so faint. But don't panic. The colder they are, the better, so to speak."

If Fiona had simply found them "like that," she would have assumed they were dead.

"Fiona, I'm going to need your help. We're going to have to drag them back to the house. Can you do that?"

Laura didn't wait for an answer.

"I'm only a few hundred feet away."

"A few hundred feet. I can't believe they didn't see the house so close by."

"When you're freezing, you get pretty confused. They probably didn't even know where they were. So listen, head straight back behind the woodshed. I'll light my flare so you can see. Got it?"

Fiona pulled on as many layers as she could while still being able to move, and threw herself into the storm. At first she couldn't see a thing, her eyes filled with tears from the cold and the wind howling seemed to have blown away her sense of direction and even her balance. Finally she made out a dim orange light through the trees and the darkness and the snow. She began plodding towards it, head down, imagining it to be the light of the angels, or God, or anything to keep her going, gritting her teeth in determination. Finally she spotted Laura, crouched down by a tree, her face lit up a ghastly orange from the flare. She looked like a demon, Fiona thought, getting ready to suck the life out of them.

Laura had left her mitts off to get a better grip on them, and she and Fiona dragged Nathaniel into the house first, since he was on top. He lay motionless on the floor, and they ran back to get Tabitha, who was considerably more difficult to shift.

Laura and Fiona had to cut through some of their clothes with scissors, as somehow the snow and the cold had turned them into stiff cardboard. Fiona pulled all the blankets she could find from the cupboards and beds and they wrapped them up right there on the floor.

"Laura, they still feel incredibly cold."

"It's called afterdrop. There's still a lot of cold there."

"Should we try to force some hot tea into them?"

"No way. If they get warmed up too fast, their blood pressure will drop too fast. Just let them warm up slowly there, under the blankets. We need to get the paramedics here as fast as possible. They need intravenous warm saline."

Nathaniel and Tabitha looked so peaceful on the floor, wrapped in their blankets, Fiona and Laura just stood and stared at them, unable to move. It was hard to tell who was more still. Finally Fiona spoke, eternally practical.

"Well, would you like some tea then?"

"I would."

Fiona began fiddling with kettles and cups, biscuits and plates, shook some sugar cubes into a crystal bowl. This was her world, everything here was familiar, comfortable, safe. She felt, at least then, ecstatically happy, having had everything that gave her life texture and form almost taken away from her and then returned.

"So how come you know all this fucking stuff?"

Laura explained her research. She explained how finding out more about the freezing and hibernation habits of frogs could have enormous benefits for human beings.

"You could preserve organs for transplants. Reduce the need for anaesthetics for surgery. All kinds of things."

"Too fucking much!"

Laura and Fiona were too busy chattering to notice that one of the figures under the blankets was beginning to stir. Nathaniel was struggling to open his eyes, and sounds began rushing into his ears, something like words but not quite words. Letters jumbled, voices, it felt as if he had been asleep for thousands of years. He tried to change position, but everything felt clamped shut, as if he had never had to use a single muscle before.

Finally Nathaniel got his eyes open and looked over at the form beside him. He tried to make a word but nothing came out, his lips twitched and his face ached. He looked down at his hands, which were now covered with tiny blisters. Where am I? he thought, but couldn't articulate. He still felt cold, as if the cold were trapped inside him, and then he noticed the hand on top of his blanket, a slender, female hand. He struggled to get his hand out from underneath the blanket, but gave up. He was so exhausted. If only he could sleep forever.

Nathaniel looked over at Tabitha. From somewhere far off he could hear his heart thumping, slowly, almost inaudibly, and the sound brought an immeasurable calm, a slow and elegant memory of a time when he had floated softly inside his mother's womb, safe, listening to the swirling sound of blood and the tapping of his heartbeat. And there they lay, for some time, Nathaniel and Tabitha drifting in and out of consciousness, as Laura and Fiona chatted over tea, and the storm passed over.

If You Find Yourself Lost, in a Place Where Frogs Are Mating

"*Frogs, I must tell you, do not give one whit for privacy. Mating will take place whether you are there or not, so if you find yourself lost, in the midst of this croaking display of male puff-uppery, it's best to ride it out, without much ado. For beneath all the noise, and the apparent chaos you have stumbled into, is a most carefully ordered world, where each call is pitched perfectly, through the ingenuity of subtle variations of sound, to that of one's mate.*"

From *Everyman's Guide to the Modern Universe and Household Management*, Nathaniel P. Speck, Professor of Medieval History, St Simons University, Chisholm, Nova Scotia

Sixteen

Nathaniel's return from the dead made him famous at the university, but it also brought with it a dog's breakfast of expectations, which made him edgy. It now seemed that he should be doing great things. During his lectures, he noticed that his students listened to him with greater attention, scribbled notes furiously, and lingered after class as if to catch a whiff of the invincibility that hung about him like a cloud. He had to choose his words more carefully, because everyone took them more seriously, and all his actions seemed heavy with portents. What does he eat for lunch – ah ha, it's lemon pudding that brings you back from the brink of death! Suddenly the local charity shop was bombarded with students buying the most flea-bitten fleeces they could find – apparel for the immortal! And books! Medieval scholarship had never loomed so large in the minds of his students, who were now trying fitfully to read between the lines for hidden clues.

Some of his students had even come up to the house, wanting to walk around the property, find the exact tree where he had slowly turned to ice, survey it for signs of death-in-the-wings, and death thwarted.

But that morning, all Nathaniel had wanted to do was head out for a quiet walk through his woods. Shaking the ice casings off the tree branches made a sound just like sleigh bells, and Nathaniel wandered about, jingling the trees. His size 12 Prospectors made huge caverns in the ice-encrusted snow, and a few joyful squirrels who had come out of hiding after the storm jumped and hopped in the troughs Nathaniel left behind as he walked, deeper and deeper into the woods which had almost claimed him, and whose branches in the wind now whispered and sighed with disappointment.

Nathaniel was trying to ignore Bill, who was trotting beside Nathaniel wagging his tail like crazy and sniffing every pine cone, every crispy leaf in amazement, no sense at all of the trouble he had caused. He kept trying to think back — when had he dropped down beside that tree? Where had he gone when his eyes closed? Was it just in his dream or had he felt the warmth of Tabitha's skin next to his penetrate through the layers of cold to where his heart, a frozen prisoner, was now slowly tapping out a message.

Nathaniel shook his head. He must have lost more than a few brain cells during that cryogenic state. He patted Bill on the head, and then asked himself why. Bill looked up, stunned. But the puzzle only lasted a few seconds, and then man and dog continued their stroll, the woods filtering the cold grey light, the clouds above frozen in position, or so it seemed, as Nathaniel looked up and wondered for a moment about the existence of heaven. Bill stopped by a withered trunk to do his doggy thing, and strained in the cold, comically intent until the deed was done, and then trotted back to Nathaniel, leaving four brown turds to freeze in the snow.

Nathaniel figured that for Bill, heaven would probably not be that different from what he had now. A warm place to sleep, food, warm trees to pee on. But not so for us, he thought, always pining away for something better, heaven bound to be, got to be, something else. Nathaniel could see ahead of him, through his icy breath and the frozen branches, a dark, semi-solid clump of trees that signalled the middle of the phalanx. He tried to picture the octagonal shape of The Hive, from the mass of lumber and scaffolding that lay strewn about.

Tabitha had begun seriously planning out Harmony right after she had been plucked from death's door by Nathaniel, the unwitting Fiona and the vastly underestimated Laura. After years of searching for its first potential occupants, she had stumbled upon them completely by accident. After that night, no one saw any good reason to leave.

Nathaniel stopped, and listened. For a few glorious moments it seemed as if the world had simply vanished, and there was only Nathaniel, and the silence, and Bill panting there at his side, unconditionally loyal, and these woods, etched with ice. He had done the right thing, letting everyone stay, even Laura's children, who would soon have their own wing at the side. It was not at all the life he imagined when he had begun writing letters to Rashida. But it was a life, one with a texture and a pattern, something original, and yet threaded invisibly to all the other lives, waking, eating, sleeping, dreaming. There was a happiness to it he couldn't explain, a sense of community, a heart turned outwards.

Suddenly Bill's ears shot up, and he stared into the darkness of The Hive, picking up something human on his doggy wavelength. Nathaniel sensed something too, and edged closer to the tangle of trees, listening. As his eyes focused, he could see bright specks of colour through the trees, something fiery red woven through the ice. He recognized Tabitha's scarf, hung like a beacon from a gnarled branch. Then he caught sight of her, hunkered down next to a pile of twigs, where she was attempting to light a small fire. At least, that was what she appeared to be doing. He stood still, and waited to see what she would do next. He didn't really think of it as spying on her, he just didn't want to startle her. Tabitha was fiddling with the sticks, rearranging them in different positions, and then standing back, cocking her head, shaking it from side to side, muttering, and then heading back towards them again, selecting different twigs, turning them over in her hands, creating a new configuration, standing back. Nathaniel wondered for a moment if she had lost even more brain cells than he had. There was a slight tremor in the breeze, the unexpected snap of a twig under his feet, and then he saw a sudden miniature storm of snow swirling at the base of a tree. He realized she was talking to herself, or more specifically, to the pile of twigs.

"I need a sign, for fuck's sake, something, anything."

Tabitha had definitely picked up a few habits from Fiona. She replaced the twigs again, peered into the pile, and then fell back into the snow.

"Fuck! I need to speak to you. How come you're never there when I need you?"

Bill and Nathaniel waited at the edge of the little island of trees, spellbound.

"Well, never mind, I'll just talk to myself then."

Tabitha sat up in the snow and warmed her hands with her breath, rubbed them together and then pulled a bar of chocolate out of her pocket. She began chomping down on the chocolate bar. Bill looked up quizzically at Nathaniel.

Nathaniel watched as Tabitha addressed her remarks to a rotting tree stump.

"Okay, it's a commune, okay? You win."

A little squall of wind swooped in, and the three of them shivered in sequence. Bill moved closer to Nathaniel, who was transfixed.

But the woods remained still. Tabitha sat alone while Nathaniel stood watching her in her cozy cocoon of trees. There was no sound but the lonely, raspy whoosh of the wind as it piped its way between the branches. Nathaniel decided to head back home with Bill. A kind of heaviness had set in, but it was not unpleasant. For so long he had been alone, and now a whole community had solidified around him.

Fiona watched Nathaniel heading towards the house, his breath puffing out ahead of him like a smoky form of Morse code. There was a pot of tea on the go, and there were some homemade biscuits pulled from the oven that very morning. Since the big chill, as Fiona had nicknamed that night, there were sources of heat and warmth everywhere at Nathaniel's, at least as far as Fiona could manage it. The coffee pot burbled and splashed all day, or sat, mildly warm on the ring, at the ready. The kettle seemed to be in constant motion, either being plugged in, or filled up, or unplugged, its steaming contents igniting the teabags in the pot. Fiona kept the fire going all day, and piled blankets like trenches everywhere.

All winter long Fiona had been haunted by a particular conversation she had had with Tabitha. She kept thinking of what Tabitha had said: "Passions stifled at one place," she had explained to Fiona, brandishing her copy of one of Fourier's more obscure texts, "reappear in another, like water held back by a dike."

"What if you don't even know what those passions are? What if you have no fucking clue?"

"You know when they're stifled, Fiona, you just know in your gut."

Fiona knew Tabitha was right. Dick had repressed and suffocated her own passions as surely as if he had covered her face with a pillow and held it there until her body went limp. In charge of domestic routines, household harmony, and the meticulous marvel of keeping a home going – that was her ecstatic centre, and Dick had not only denied it, he had mocked it. But what about these counter passions, as Fourier had named them? What about the water gushing out of the dike for fuck's sake? She couldn't escape the idea that now gripped her mind. If her own passions had been suppressed, what on earth had been squeezed out from under the mat? What slithering creature had arrived at Nathaniel's doorstep, and what trouble had she caused! He had been a saint to let her in! But then Nathaniel, he celebrated Fiona's passion. Nothing was peevishly denied an existence because it was politically incorrect.

By now Nathaniel had returned from his walk in the woods, and was standing by the back door shaking the snow off his boots. Fiona greeted him with a steaming cup of mulled cider and Nathaniel replied with an easy grin. Nathaniel had credited Fiona and Laura for saving his life, and it just wasn't in his heart to hold Fiona responsible for launching all the trouble in the first place, chasing after Bill. They were a community now, the phalanx taking concrete shape with Tabitha at the helm. Construction had begun on the Central Hive, and large parcels of treed land had been cleared for building over the winter. The idea had even taken root beyond the confines of academia. The President of the local Farmer's League had come forward to support the whole notion of agricultural association, many of them having been nearly wiped out by the hoppers and desperately trying to get back on their feet. Working together, twenty farmers could save themselves a lot of trouble. Nathaniel promised them the northeast corner of Tabitha's property, to establish orchards and corn fields. They could see, just as well as Fourier, that trying to run twenty rundown farms separately made no sense, when if they pooled their resources they could run one big well-appointed farm, share the crop and the profits, and save themselves both time and money.

"Of course, we're not too sure about all this hippy commune nonsense, you understand. Free love and all. But we can work the land."

"One step at a time, Cameron, one step at a time."

Nathaniel was still blowing and sipping his cider and thinking back to this conversation when Laura walked in, and he offered her some of his, seeing her reddened cheeks and watery eyes. She declined with a wave of her hands, and Nathaniel was surprised again, the way he always was, by the sight of those hands close up, now missing several fingers as a result of the frostbite suffered that night. The three of them wandered silently into the living room and plopped into their respective chairs. They often said very little, but there had arisen a kind of comfort in each other's company, a sense of knowing what the other needed or wanted.

Nathaniel looked over at Fiona, who had closed her eyes and was about to veer off into nap land. He too felt his eyes beginning to close, an unhurried silence filling the room, the quirky little sounds of Bill snoring at Fiona's feet being the only interruption to a strange little peace that had descended on Nathaniel's house. Laura wandered off to lie down in her room. Plans were posted on the walls of her room for a children's wing, to be added on at the back of the house, overlooking a field of pumpkins where the children of Harmony could run and play. The runaway success of Twisted's mail-order franchise operation would likely fund Harmony for years to come, at least until the phalanx was on its feet and running.

By the time Nathaniel woke up, it was already dark and he got up and bustled about, turning on lights and putting kindling in the fireplace, rooting around with his poker. It had become like an evening prayer, putting the fire together, gathering the kindling and sticks, coaxing the flames with the bellows, watching the room fill with the amber glow. It was, Nathaniel supposed, the closest thing he would ever get to religion, a sense of God and the rightness of things in the world. The snapping of sticks and the smell of the smoke burrowed Fiona out of her sleepy den, and she watched Nathaniel at the fire, like a great bear fending off the elements and the wilderness of a cold grate.

"Nathaniel, you are a fucking wonder."

Nathaniel turned around and laughed, a deep resonant laugh that echoed off the walls.

"Indeed. And did you think I would lie there and let you freeze?"

Since the storm, many of their conversations now seemed laced with irony.

Nathaniel went off into the kitchen and prepared a pot of tea, and a plate of sandwiches, about as domestic as he got, but it was an improvement that didn't go unappreciated. They sat round the fire, munching and sipping and watching the flames.

"Do you think she's still asleep?"

Fiona had broken into the silence like a bull.

"I think so. She hauled a lot of wood today."

Nathaniel sat back in his chair and waited for Fiona to continue.

"Well, being here and chopping wood is a lot better for Laura than having her passion suffocated."

Fiona's remark took Nathaniel by surprise, unused as he was to having Fiona spout Fourier around the house. It even surprised Fiona herself, who then began frantically knitting, the umpteenth afghan she was making for the house. She spoke again.

"You know, it's what anyone would have done, gone out in a storm to look for their dog." Fiona surprised herself, as if her private thoughts had suddenly tumbled out by accident. "I'm not a fucking idiot."

Fiona had finally told Nathaniel that it was she who had convinced Tabitha to leave the university and head home. Fiona continued knitting, frantically. Nathaniel's kindness to her, and her own stupidity in making that phone call the day of the storm had brought with it a huge and claustrophobic guilt. Bill wasn't a child, after all, he was a dog. And she hadn't intended for Nathaniel to go out looking for her. She had no idea. And she had thought that Tabitha would be safer at home, she really had. How long was she expected to suffocate all this guilt? The needles clacked and her hands whirled like tops. What counter passion would result? She couldn't stand it any longer. She flung the knitting off her lap, where it woke Bill from a happy slumber, and he snorted and began pawing at the wool.

"Are you going to ask me to leave? I don't belong in a fucking commune! I'm a fucking fake!" And with that she ran from the room and collapsed on her bed, the tears coming out in racking sobs. Laura had come in at that moment, rubbing her eyes sleepily and hearing those last few words. Nathaniel and Laura looked at each other, and without saying anything walked together to Fiona's room, and covered her with a blanket. Tabitha joined them and they lay down beside her, and the four of them fell asleep. There they stayed, until the sun was well past the midpoint the next day, and the fire had gone cold in the grate, and something dark and slithery was purged from Fiona's soul.

The next spring, Tabitha came up behind Nathaniel in his study and put her hands on his shoulders. "There's something I want to show you."

Nathaniel didn't seem to mind being interrupted, and he turned and followed her to the kitchen, where their coats and boots waited in a neat series along the wall.

Tabitha had discovered the pond in the middle of the winter, frozen over like a dark green sheet of glass and dusted with snow. Circling the pond, surprised by its circumference and the spell it seemed to cast, she had thought about how the ice had crept in from the shore, edging towards the centre until one day everything had been frozen over and sealed in, the frogs and turtles curled in the mud well below the pond's surface, the fish moving in slow motion through the green water.

How like a heart, she thought, on those thoughtful days, how like a life, gradually freezing over and sealing up everything inside, waiting for a thaw, a spring, another chance. She had peered with fascination at the pond's green mirror, and wondered why she had said nothing to Nathaniel all winter long about her feelings. Maybe, somewhere at her frozen core, she didn't feel she deserved love at all. Perhaps she'd slowed her heartbeat down for too long, something fundamental had died off during that particularly gruelling winter. Tabitha had tapped at the pond's edge with a stick for an answer, sending out a frantic little Morse code to the confused fish below, but got nothing.

But now it was spring, and the surface was bustling with insect larvae chasing each other like children playing tag. Red-winged blackbirds staked out cattails and frogs scrambled to the surface to sniff out mates and the spring air.

A rustle in the undergrowth produced Bill, out chasing rabbits, and infatuated in that doggie way with the idea of spring returning. He'd jumped and clambered over fallen trees, rotting logs, and boulders, to get there, delighted with the puddles and the dirt and the arrival of new smells. Once he spotted Tabitha he stopped suddenly and then he listened. For rising from that scummy, covered-over-with-vegetation, and prickly-with-cattails pond, came the unmistakable, screeching, monotonous, high-pitched, ear-splitting din of frogs sending out their mating calls.

Nathaniel marvelled at the ground, all spongy underfoot, setting everything up to get born again. The moisture had travelled up the sides and toes of his Prospectors and crept in where the stitches were not perfectly secure and the leather had worn down to nothing. But it didn't seem to bother him. Working the land seemed to have given Nathaniel a kind of special claim over it, and everything that went with it, rot, mould, damp woolly socks. He spotted Laura, jotting down notes at the far end of the pond. He raised his voice above the deafening frogs.

"Laura! Hello! Have you seen the children?"

"Over here, with Fiona. They're mesmerized by the frogs, I think." Her two boys were peering into the water, pointing and laughing. Fiona stood behind, protectively, one hand on each of their shoulders, steadying them.

Tabitha stood in front of the pond, one foot slowly sinking into the oozing mud.

"Come over here. I want to ask you something."

Bill trotted over to meet Nathaniel, and then trotted stupidly back with him, tail wagging all the while, full of doggy excitement and not knowing why or about what. The three of them stood at the pond's edge, listening to the frogs. Something about the din made Nathaniel fidgety, all that brazen, chest-baring, no-holds-barred noise to signal for a mate; so undignified, and yet stirring all the same. Tabitha had to shout to be heard, they were so close to the pond's edge. Nathaniel leaned closer to hear her, and sensed the warmth of her body, caught a sweet smell like a new rain, and the excitement which seemed to light up her face like a candle. He breathed her in, felt his pulse rocket.

"This is it. Laura's Research Centre for the Study of Cryobiology."

They had talked about it vaguely over the winter, setting up something for Laura, who pined for the academic work that had long held her in its slimy, green grip.

"Do you think this is really what she has in mind?"

"I think this is exactly what she has in mind." Tabitha tried abstractedly to extract herself from the sucking brown muck beneath her. "A natural habitat. I mean, if you're into frogs, this is the fucking place to be."

"I'm glad to see Fiona has taught you well." Nathaniel laughed, and then immediately regretted it, because he thought it might seem to trivialize what Tabitha was trying to explain. "I think I just had a different picture in my mind of a research centre."

"No, really. I think this little pond will be Laura's idea of heaven. And just think, all this research can go on right here, in our little phalanx."

Something about the way Tabitha said "our little phalanx" set Nathaniel's heart on fire. The possibilities began leaping before him like water striders across the pond. Tabitha's eyes were big with excitement, and Nathaniel noticed for the first time since she had come into his life they were as deep and green as the pond itself. He longed, as he had longed all winter, to take her in his arms and tell her what she had released that frozen night. But, as he had done all winter, he simply stayed put, because no matter what had taken place, no matter what new-found identity he had taken on following not only a miraculous escape from death but a seemingly uncanny ability to attract women into his life, at the core he still felt like Nathaniel Speck, a man unlikely to find a bride except by the catalogue method, and even that hadn't worked. His heart began to slow down again. Tabitha was babbling about the central dining hall.

"How about another octagonal shape? And what about having pathways leading out from each window to different sections of the community – this way to the libraries, this way to the orchards, you know, like a wheel."

Nathaniel and Tabitha had had many conversations like this over the long months of winter, the business of shaping and moulding an idea steering them through winter like a bright beacon always just ahead of them. Somehow the phalanx had entered into all of their lives like a mysterious healing force.

"Listen to that one. Can you hear it? Spring Peeper. Sounds like crazed sleigh bells." Tabitha had closed her eyes and was listening intently to the racket.

"Pseudacris crucifer. The ears of the female Spring Peeper are tuned exactly to the midpoint of the pitch of the male Peeper's call."

Nathaniel couldn't help it. After talking to Laura about her research he'd done a little reading on the subject of frogs, and he'd been out to the pond with his meters and tuning forks, taking readings. Tabitha looked at him in her usual amazement.

"How can you keep all this stuff in your head? It makes sense though, doesn't it. How else is she going to hear her true love in all this noise?"

"Indeed."

Nathaniel and Tabitha stood quietly for a while, the air around them vibrating, buzzing, and humming with sound, redwinged blackbirds teetering on the tips of precarious-looking cattails, the sun beginning to set, a purple fire in the distance.

Tabitha pulled a rock from the mud beneath her and threw it into the pond, for emphasis, then wondered if she'd bopped an unsuspecting pseudacris crucifer on the head by accident. Bill looked frantically from right to left, wondering where the sound came from. She pulled her jacket closer around her neck and fastened the buttons.

"You know why people are drawn to Utopias like fucking moths, don't you?"

The darkness was collapsing around them like a tent, and the sound of the frogs was beginning to give him a headache. But Tabitha had chosen this moment to embark on what felt like the most intimate conversation they'd ever had. So Nathaniel stayed put, and thrust his hands deep inside his pockets for warmth. He took a stab at her question.

"Because they want to believe that, given the right conditions, human beings could be perfect?"

Nathaniel waited for Tabitha's revelation.

"Because they want to believe they can start again."

The air seemed to tremble for the longest time as neither of them said anything. A rush of birds swarmed overhead.

"I used to talk to my mother out here, you know. Or at least, she used to talk to me. Do you believe in ghosts?"

Nathaniel thought back to the afternoon of the twigs. "I believe you."

"I think she's on sabbatical right now though." Tabitha chuckled at her little joke, and shivered. "Haven't seen her for ages." The frogs droned on.

"I picture her up there though, somewhere, don't you?" Weeks and months of clearing land, chopping down trees, and meditating with Laura and her half-frozen frogs, had made Tabitha unexpectedly prone to soul-searching. She longed for Nathaniel to put his arm around her, but then she realized it would probably never happen.

"Nathaniel, there's something I've been wanting to tell you." Tabitha turned away, fighting back a wave of nervousness. Nathaniel's deep, rumbling, velvet voice broke right through the cacophony of peeps, screeches and burbles. He took her by the shoulders and turned her towards him again. "I know, in fact..." pulling Tabitha tight to his chest, Nathaniel forgot for one blazing moment to be Nathaniel Speck, "there's been something I wanted to tell you."

Tabitha buried her face for a long time in the huge musty warmth of Nathaniel's chest. The partially constructed hive, illuminated by the setting sun in the distance, was like a strange temple, the shape of an idea pieced together unsteadily with ladders, ropes, and wooden beams. From a distance the scaffolding on either side appeared like two arms reaching towards the heavens. Soon the sun would disappear behind the trees and the frogs, hundreds of wide-eyed, big-mouthed, slimy heartthrobs, would be croaking as loudly as their hearts could bear.